7-14

SPECIAL MESSAGE TO READERS

This book is published by
THE ULVERSCROFT FOUNDATION
a registered charity in the U.K., No. 264873

The Foundation was established in 1974 to provide funds to help towards research, diagnosis and treatment of eye diseases. Below are a few examples of contributions made by THE ULVERSCROFT FOUNDATION:

A new Children's Assessment Unit
at Moorfield's Hospital, London.

●

Twin operating theatres at the
Western Ophthalmic Hospital, London.

●

The Frederick Thorpe Ulverscroft Chair of
Ophthalmology at the University of Leicester.

●

Eye Laser equipment to various eye hospitals.

If you would like to help further the work of the Foundation by making a donation or leaving a legacy, every contribution, no matter how small, is received with gratitude. Please write for details to:

THE ULVERSCROFT FOUNDATION,
**The Green, Bradgate Road, Anstey,
Leicester LE7 7FU. England
Telephone: (0533)364325**

I've travelled the world twice over,
Met the famous: saints and sinners,
Poets and artists, kings and queens,
Old stars and hopeful beginners,
I've been where no-one's been before,
Learned secrets from writers and cooks
All with one library ticket
To the wonderful world of books.

DEATH'S LONG SHADOW

A relatively unknown but prestigious College in the centre of Oxford is bombed, but there are no indications that terrorists of the usual kind have been responsible. Chief Inspector Tansey of the Thames Valley Police Force integrates himself into College life and interviews undergraduates and dons, one of whom has faced the most dangerous dilemma of his life. The investigation is fraught with danger, and it is only after shrewd detection that Tansey is able to bring it to its unexpected conclusion.

Books by John Penn
in the Ulverscroft Large Print Series:

NOTICE OF DEATH
DECEITFUL DEATH
A DEADLY SICKNESS
UNTO THE GRAVE
A WILL TO KILL
MORTAL TERM
BARREN REVENGE
ACCIDENT PRONE
OUTRAGEOUS EXPOSURES
A KILLING TO HIDE

JOHN PENN

DEATH'S LONG SHADOW

Complete and Unabridged

ULVERSCROFT
Leicester

First published in Great Britain in 1991 by
HarperCollins Publishers
London

First Large Print Edition
published October 1993
by arrangement with
HarperCollins Publishers
London

British Library CIP Data

Penn, John
    Death's long shadow.—Large print ed.—
    Ulverscroft large print series: mystery
    I. Title
    823.914 [F]

    ISBN 0–7089–2959–1

Published by
F. A. Thorpe (Publishing) Ltd.
Anstey, Leicestershire

Set by Words & Graphics Ltd.
Anstey, Leicestershire
Printed and bound in Great Britain by
T. J. Press (Padstow) Ltd., Padstow, Cornwall

This book is printed on acid-free paper

This book is fiction. Any relationship between the characters in this novel and any person who exists in reality is purely coincidental. Apologies are offered to Lincoln College, Oxford, for depriving it of part of its territory.

1

AT one moment Jean White was in a deep sleep. The next she was fully awake. She lay still, breathing carefully. She could feel her heart thumping. In the twin bed beside her, Greg, her husband, emitted gentle snores. Slowly Jean opened her eyes.

The curtains were partly drawn back to allow a gentle breeze to blow through the open window into the room, and by the light of the night sky Jean could see the familiar objects around her. She relaxed. She had thought that some noise, some unwelcome sound, had woken her, but now she told herself that she must have been feeling the effects of a menacing dream.

Then the noise was repeated. But this time Jean was awake and the sound didn't frighten her. She knew that there was someone downstairs and she assumed that it was her daughter, Rosemary. She glanced at the clock on the bedside table.

Its illuminated hands pointed to three o'clock.

Three o'clock! Jean threw back the duvet and got out of bed. She was angry. Against her better judgement she had agreed that Rosemary might go to a birthday party with Tony Pulent, the son of their next door neighbour. Rosemary had sworn she would be home by twelve-thirty. In Jean's opinion this was far too late for a girl of sixteen who had to be at school the following day, but Rosemary had pleaded that this was a special occasion, and it had been difficult to refuse her.

And Greg had been no help. Jean frowned at her husband's sleeping form as she slid her feet into slippers, pulled on a robe, and brushed back her short, dark hair. He had said that she shouldn't fuss, that Rosemary was a sensible girl and Tony a responsible boy. Of course he was right, but what he didn't seem to realize was that his daughter looked at least two years older than her age and had become an extremely attractive young woman. As for Tony, it wasn't a great demonstration of his much-vaunted responsibility to keep Rosemary out until the small hours like this.

Seething with anger, Jean opened the bedroom door and started along the corridor. The moon shone through an uncurtained window and she had no need to switch on a light. The north Oxford house was comparatively modern — Greg's parents had helped them to buy it twenty years ago when they had got married on the strength of Greg's election to a Fellowship at St Xavier's College — and Jean knew that no squeaky boards would betray her. She planned to surprise Tony and Rosemary and tell them precisely what she thought of their behaviour.

There were more sounds from below. Jean stopped. By chance she was standing by Rosemary's bedroom door and, as the sounds downstairs ceased, she heard other gentler sounds that were not quite snores coming from her daughter's room. Her heart began to thump again. Carefully she turned the handle and opened the door a few inches so that she could see inside.

Rosemary was in bed. She was lying

on her back, her mouth slightly open, her dark hair framing a pretty face that in sleep looked surprisingly childish and vulnerable. She stirred and Jean quickly shut the door and leant against it.

Jean White was not normally a nervous woman, but there had been several burglaries in the neighbourhood recently, in one of which the householder, an elderly woman, had been beaten up so badly as to require eight weeks of hospital treatment. Jean had no desire to face violent men by herself. She crept back to the bedroom she shared with Greg.

Greg was still asleep. He was tired. He had had a wearying week and the previous day, although a Sunday, had not been a day of rest as far as he was concerned. It was just after the beginning of the Michaelmas Term and therefore of the University year — always a difficult time with the influx of new undergraduates who had to be welcomed to the college and settled into a way of work that was strange to many of them, used as they often were to much stricter supervision at their schools.

Further, there were innumerable

administrative details to be attended to, and personal problems to be faced and solved. In a small college such as St Xavier's a Fellow and tutor was expected to deal with everything from homesickness or the need for a particular diet to a request to read a different subject from the one for which the student had been awarded an exhibition.

On the whole, Greg enjoyed his work. He was a good teacher, and he was interested in those he taught. His lectures were always well attended, and if some of his less popular colleagues claimed that this was because he was a good-looking man, over six foot and with an attractive manner — he didn't give a damn. He made no effort to set out to please. And for the most part his students achieved their potentials, which was often more than was expected of them.

Jean complained that he spent too much time on student affairs and college matters, to the detriment of his academic career, and it was true that he had published very little; what was intended to become a *magnum opus* on Milton — his subject was English literature — remained unfinished after five years. But Greg was not ambitious, which was why he did his best to shun involvement in the intricate backbiting that inevitably characterized the internal politics of all colleges. In this way he saved himself a lot of hassle, though sometimes, when he was not present, he found that decisions of which he did not approve had been made for him. Something like this had happened just before the beginning of term. Dr Cathcart, who was responsible for teaching English language at St Xavier's, had collapsed with peritonitis and was expected to be away for some weeks. Who was to take on his work? Greg ignored the ensuing wrangle, only to discover that Cathcart's first-year students had been assigned to him — thus adding to his workload.

"Too much," he muttered in his sleep. "Can't remember — damned stuff. Years since I did any Anglo-Saxon. Too much. Got my own."

Irritably he twitched away as Jean shook him by the shoulder. He mumbled something else that she didn't catch and she shook him harder. "What — is — it?" he demanded sleepily. He wished she would go away. He had no desire to wake up. In his dream he had been telling Sir Philip Pinel, Master of St Xavier's College, Oxford, that he refused to be imposed upon, that he'd got more than enough to do without taking over —

"Greg! For God's sake wake up, Greg!"

"All right, darling."

Greg White forced himself awake. He sat up in bed and yawned. Then he smiled at his wife. He took in the fact that she was wearing her robe, and suddenly her anxiety communicated itself to him.

"What is it, Jean? Isn't Rosemary home yet?"

"Not so loud, Greg. No, it's not Rosemary. She's in bed asleep, as she ought to be at three in the morning. But there's someone downstairs. I heard them moving around. I thought it might be Rosemary and Tony but it's not. We've got burglars."

"Damn!" Greg threw back his duvet and slid his legs over the side of the bed.

7

Then he said, in a loud whisper, "Are you sure, Jean? I can't hear anyone."

"Quite sure!" Jean bit off the words. "We ought to get the police."

"How can we? The phone's downstairs. I always said we should have one by the bed too."

"So what can we do?"

"We certainly can't phone anyone." Without thinking, Greg had put on his dressing-gown and slippers. It was stupid but it made him feel slightly less defenceless. He looked about the room. "There's not a thing up here that would do as a weapon, not even a golf club."

"You're not going down?"

"There's not much choice, is there? I'll put on all the lights as I go and make a lot of noise. With luck they'll run."

"For heaven's sake, Greg! They didn't run from old Mrs Porteous. They beat her up. She was in hospital for eight weeks."

"I'm not a feeble old lady. Besides, we don't know that these are the same chaps."

"They could be. The police never caught the others. Greg, it's not worth

8

it. We've scarcely anything that can't be replaced and we're insured."

"Underinsured. But that's not the point."

Greg would have found it difficult to explain exactly what the point was. He didn't think of himself as a brave man, but nor did he consider himself a coward. He didn't want to go downstairs and possibly confront a couple of violent louts equipped with knives and knuckle-dusters. On the other hand some atavistic instinct was prompting him to do just that.

"Greg, please don't — "

"Jean, I must — "

The frantically whispered argument reached no conclusion. It was interrupted by a shrill scream of terror, abruptly cut off. Greg and Jean froze. Then they ran, fear for Rosemary overwhelming any fear for themselves.

Greg was quicker than Jean. He dashed into the corridor ahead of her — and stopped. Jean, who couldn't see round him, ran into his back. He half-turned, reached behind him and took her hand, pulling her close to him.

"Stay exactly where you are," a voice said.

The voice was without noticeable accent, though not especially well-spoken. Its source was clearly to be seen in the light through the window — a stocky, broad-shouldered man, about five feet nine in height, with a round head and rather short legs. He was dressed completely in black — black shoes, black trousers and jacket, black gloves and a black stocking pulled over his face to disguise his features and render him unrecognizable. He exuded a sense of purpose, emphasized by the serviceable-looking revolver he held in a firm grip.

"Oh God!" Greg heard Jean mutter. She was clutching his hand tightly. "Greg, where's Rosemary?"

Her question was answered without Greg's intervention. A second man had appeared in the doorway of Rosemary's bedroom. He was dressed like his companion, but was taller and thinner and gave the impression of being the younger of the two. He was pushing Rosemary in front of him. He had bent her arms behind her back and he had the muzzle of a small automatic pistol pressed against her neck.

"Dad! Mum!" Rosemary whimpered. In her short woollen dressing-gown and bare feet she looked like the child she was. "He's hurting me!"

Greg started forward. "Leave her alone, damn you!" he cried.

"Stay where you are!" the older man snapped. "And listen carefully. If you do what you're told you won't be harmed, any of you, but we're not fooling — and you'd better believe it."

"Very well." Greg controlled himself with difficulty. "But let my daughter go."

The older man nodded to his companion, who released Rosemary. The girl ran to Greg and pressed herself against him. She was sobbing, but stopped almost at once as he fondled her hair.

"It's all right, darling. Be brave."

"I'll try." Rosemary found a handkerchief and blew her nose hard.

With his family close to him Greg was less inclined to be amenable. He confronted the two men. "Who the hell

11

are you? And what do you want?" he demanded.

His belligerence had no effect. The older, shorter man, who was clearly in charge, merely gestured with his gun. "You're to follow me downstairs. Slowly. Don't try any tricks. My — my mate will be behind you and he won't hesitate to shoot. Nor will I."

Somehow, in spite of his vicious tone, Greg wasn't convinced that the men would shoot. But it was not a judgement he could risk. He tried a last protest.

"Now, look here. Just let us go back to the bedroom. There's nothing worth taking there. Steal what you like in the rest of the house. We shan't try to stop you."

This approach elicited no response, except a repetition of the order to go downstairs. Greg could feel the pressure of Jean's hand on his back, urging him forward. There seemed no alternative, and the strange little party with its stranger escort went meekly down the stairs to the front hall.

"Into the dining-room," the man leading them ordered, and there was satisfaction in his voice.

The dining-room in the Whites' house was at the rear, overlooking the garden. It was not a big room. The oval table would seat some six in comfort, and eight with care; they rarely had eight people in for a formal meal. Jean preferred to give casual buffet parties which, as there was always plenty of wine and the food was excellent, were very popular.

When Greg and Jean had gone to bed the door to the dining-room had been shut for the night. Now it was open, the curtains drawn close and the light on. The chairs around the table had been rearranged, so that three of them were on one side, facing the curtained window, and the other five pushed back against the wall.

"Sit down! The girl in the middle, between you."

They obeyed. Later Greg was asked why they had submitted so tamely. The question annoyed him. What else could they have done? The surprise, the guns, the disbelief in what was happening had numbed them all. And yes, they were afraid. The men might not want to kill,

13

but they had shown that they wouldn't hesitate to hurt, possibly maim, if they didn't get what they wanted. And what the hell did they want? They were no ordinary thieves — that was for certain.

"Hold out your hands, palms facing."

Again they obeyed and, while the shorter man kept them covered, the other produced from a bag — previously unnoticed in a corner of the room — a collection of handcuffs. It took him a minute to fix them on. Then he got down under the table.

"Ankles together!"

Greg felt the cold metal against his flesh and heard the snap of the cuffs. Then the man went to Jean; Greg saw her shift in her chair. Neither of them had protested. But Rosemary cried out and tried to push herself away from the table.

"No! No! Don't! Leave me alone!"

"What is it, darling?"

"He was — was trying to — to touch me up, Mum."

"You filthy beast!" Greg staggered to his feet. "Don't you dare lay another finger on her or I — "

14

"Or you'll what?" The man had emerged from beneath the table, and it was obvious, in spite of his stocking mask, that he was grinning broadly. "Or you'll what?" he repeated.

And Greg, feeling sick, knew he had no answer. If he had been going to act, he should have acted before, though God knew what he might have achieved. Now, at least for the moment, he was helpless.

2

THE two men stood in the doorway of the dining-room, muttering to each other. Greg studied his manacled hands. He felt deflated and useless, unable even to offer encouragement to Jean or Rosemary. Rosemary was making an unsuccessful effort to curl herself up into a ball and Jean, who was the most lightly clad of the three of them, had begun to shiver. The muttering ceased.

The younger man left the room, but returned at once. "Do any of you take sugar?"

Sugar! In the circumstances it seemed the most irrelevant of questions and no one answered.

"In your tea," the man said patiently. "I'm going to make us tea." He spoke as if he were explaining something simple to a group of mentally deficients.

Jean found her voice. "No. None of us take sugar but — but we'd love some

16

tea. It's cold in here and we're only wearing our nightclothes." She hesitated. "There's a thermostat in the hall. Would you please turn it up?"

"Oke!"

Jean, with her placatory manner, was achieving more than he was, Greg thought, as the man departed and a click indicated that he had turned up the central heating as she had asked. But the situation was incredible — two characters, two presumed villains, who were prepared to make tea for their — their victims? What in God's name did they want? Then he remembered old Mrs Porteous and he was fearful, for Rosemary and Jean — and for himself — but especially for Rosemary. He stared intently at the masked gunman who was sitting across the room from him.

"Tell me what you want!"

"Later."

But Greg felt a need to make him talk. "You're not common burglars?"

"No!"

"Bank robbers. Abingdon."

Rosemary had spoken in a whisper and the man gave no sign that he had heard.

Greg gave his daughter a startled glance. Could she be right? He knew what she meant. A few months ago the family of a bank manager in Abingdon had been held hostage at gunpoint while he was forced to drive to the bank and open the safe for the thieves. Something had gone wrong, a teller had alerted the police and the would-be robbers had been caught. But crimes were often copied. This might be an example, except —

"Did you hear what my daughter said? Are you hoping to rob a bank? Because if you are you're out of luck. You've come to the wrong house. I'm a don, a university teacher. Mr Pulent, who *is* a bank manager, lives next door."

There was a hoot of laughter from the taller man, who had returned carrying a tray with three mugs of tea on it. He placed one in front of each of the Whites, who had to manage as best they could with their handcuffed wrists.

"Yours is in the kitchen, boss. I've had some."

"Ta! We'll have a talk when I get back." The older man addressed Greg. "Meantime, the answer's no. We aren't planning to rob a bank, and we didn't come to the wrong house. It's you we need to help us — Mr White."

"How on earth can I help you? Since you know who I am you must know I told you the truth. I'm just a teacher at St Xavier's."

"Later! Drink your tea before it gets cold."

Rosemary giggled hysterically. "That's just what Mum used to say when I was small."

"It's good advice, darling." Jean was already struggling to lift her mug.

Greg marvelled at his wife's resilience. Now that she had got over the first shock Jean seemed to be accepting the situation. He wished he could be so sanguine. Perhaps it had been too much to hope that this couple of unspeakable but curious customers had mistaken him for his neighbour, but at least it would have made some sense. His imagination boggled when he tried to think of what he could possibly do for them that would warrant this treatment of himself and his family. But it was useless to speculate. Presumably he would soon be told. With difficulty he lifted his mug between his manacled hands and drank. The tea was surprisingly comforting.

★ ★ ★

The man whom the other addressed as boss returned to the dining-room. He drew up a chair and sat at the table. His companion lounged in the doorway, but his gun was ready and he was watchful. They were taking no chances.

"I'm going to ask you some questions, and I want straight answers." The man opposite them looked from Greg to Rosemary to Jean and back to Greg. "Cooperate and you'll come to no harm, as I said. You've my word for it. But try to trick us and you'll be sorry. You've my word for that too. Do you understand?"

They nodded in unison, without speaking. They understood that the threat was real — but that was all.

"First you, Rosemary. Today's Monday. You expect to go to school, don't you?" He didn't wait for an answer. "Well, you won't be going today. You'll be staying at home with your mother. What happens when you miss a day?"

"I — I don't know what you mean." She resented the patronizing way in which he was questioning her.

"You must miss a day sometimes," he said patiently, "when you have a cold or just feel sick."

"Mother telephones my housemistress. If I'm away more than a few days — "

"You won't be. You'll be at school tomorrow — if your father's sensible." He turned to Jean. "What time would you phone, Mrs White?"

"About eight forty-five."

"You'll do that, then." It was an order. "Now, what had you planned for today?"

Jean hesitated. "Nothing much. Monday's washing day as a rule." She stopped, fighting for control. Her simple, mundane statement had brought their predicament home to her. What *was* she doing? How could she be thinking of clothes washing when she and Greg and Rosemary were sitting in their own dining-room, bound hand and foot and menaced by a couple of armed thugs? It was absurd but — she mustn't appear hostile. "A dull day," she concluded.

"You haven't arranged to go out anywhere?" And when Jean shook her head. "Are you expecting anyone to come to the house?"

"No. No one."

"What about the milkman, the postman — other deliveries?"

"The bottles are by the side door. The milkman only rings on Fridays, when he's paid. The postman puts the letters through the box. If it's a parcel he'll ring but if there's no answer he'll leave it in the back porch. I'm not expecting anyone else, except the newspaper boy, but he'll put the papers through the letter box too."

Why am I telling him all this? Jean wondered. It's stupid. Now he knows that he can do what he likes with us because no one will come to help. But he had said they wouldn't be hurt, that Rosemary would be at school tomorrow, and somehow she believed him. Of course he had also said that it depended on Greg. She glanced sideways at her husband, who gave her a wry smile. Whatever they wanted of him he wouldn't refuse, she thought. He would do it — whatever it was — for Rosemary's sake, and hers.

"That's oke then, Mrs White. Mr White?"

"Me? You want to know about my day? Well, first of all I'm due at the regular Monday morning meeting in the Master's Lodgings at St Xavier's at nine-thirty. The meeting will probably last a couple of hours or more, depending on the length of the agenda. Then the Master will offer us a sherry — "

"Enough, Mr White. It's not going to be like that. Not this Monday morning. We have other plans for you."

"I gathered you might have." Greg was grim. "I only wish you'd tell me what they are. I assume you'll want my wife to phone the College to say I'm ill. I won't mind that. I find these meetings extraordinarily tedious and I'll be glad of a chance to miss one."

There was no immediate response as Greg stopped speaking, and the silence lengthened. It had the effect of making Greg feel foolish. He glared at the man opposite him.

23

Suddenly the man said, "You must dress now."

"Dress? What about washing and shaving?"

"We'll look after all that, Mr White. My — my mate here will remove your cuffs and take you upstairs. But don't try any funny business. Remember, I'll be down here keeping an eye on your wife and your daughter. A smashed shoulder wouldn't be much fun for a young girl."

Greg nodded; he couldn't bring himself to speak. He had no means of knowing if there was any substance in the threat. But the threat was enough by itself. He couldn't risk Rosemary being shot, and probably pointlessly.

He was escorted up to the bedroom and bathroom, where the younger man watched as he took off his dressing-gown and his pyjama jacket. He washed briefly and shaved with his electric razor. He glanced at his companion and took the opportunity to use the lavatory. Then he returned to the bedroom to put on underpants, clean shirt, trousers, tie, sweater, jacket, socks, shoes. He combed his hair. He slipped on his watch and filled his pockets with the usual assortment of articles that he kept overnight on a small tray on his chest of drawers. All he needed was his briefcase, he thought, and he could have set off for the College; no one would have noticed anything amiss or unusual. But for what was he ready?

It was a surprise when, as soon as they returned to the dining-room, the older man ordered him to sit down again at the table, and his ankles, though not his hands, were manacled. Because he was dressed and Jean and Rosemary were still in their nightclothes he felt alienated from them, as if he had taken an unfair advantage. He glanced at his watch. It was past seven. He had heard the grandfather clock in the hall strike while he was dressing, but had miscounted and thought it had struck six. It was hard to believe that the time, which had borne so little relation to reality since Jean had woken him, had passed so quickly.

"Now breakfast," said the older man.

There was a gasp from Rosemary. In spite of the extraordinary circumstances, the threats and the fear, she was hungry. She hoped that the suggestion of breakfast wasn't a malicious joke, but a genuine offer.

"Are you proposing to cook it for us?" Jean asked coldly. Seeing Greg dressed as if ready to depart somewhere, she felt her fears for Rosemary and herself magnify.

"Tea and toast only, and make the most of it. It may be some time before you get anything else."

"What do you mean by that, damn it? Stop talking in riddles! Tell us — tell *me* what you want!" Greg banged a fist on the table. "One moment you utter appalling threats, the next you make us tea, offer us breakfast. It makes no sense. What the hell do you want?"

"Later, Mr White, as I said before."

"No! Now! Tell me now, or you can stuff your breakfast."

"You've decided not to cooperate? You intend to be difficult?"

"I want to know — "

"Oke. That'll be breakfast for two then as Mr White and his family don't want any. Sure you won't change your mind, Mr White?"

"Dad, please! He said it might be ages

before we got anything else — all day, perhaps."

"Greg, for heaven's sake! What have we got to lose?"

Greg drew a deep breath. What *had* they got to lose? Pride maybe, but that was already lost. Nevertheless, he felt that every time they obeyed a simple order or accepted a favour they were weakening their will to resist and putting themselves even more at the mercy of the two thugs who menaced them. Yet what was the alternative? To deprive Jean and Rosemary of a cup of tea and a slice of toast that they might well be grateful for later seemed a pretty worthless act.

"All right. Forget what I said. We'd like breakfast."

"Good. That's sensible of you, Mr White."

"Don't you think you might free my wife and daughter's hands so that they can eat decently, and enjoy the meal you're so kindly providing?" Greg tried to combine irony with a little authority.

"No call to be sarcastic, Mr White. They can manage. It doesn't matter if they spill a bit on themselves. It's

27

different for you. We wouldn't want you going to your College with marmalade down your tie, would we?"

Greg said nothing. The altercation over the breakfast hadn't achieved much, but at least he had gathered one piece of information. They intended him to go to St Xavier's. He knew better than to ask why.

★ ★ ★

Time passed. Breakfast arrived, was eaten and the dirty plates and mugs removed. No one attempted to make conversation. They were all growing tired; strain and lack of sleep were beginning to tell on them. But the two men, who had taken turns to eat in the kitchen, didn't relax their vigilance.

There were several minor alarms. The milkman's cheery whistle and the clank of his bottles made them stiffen, as did the thud of the newspapers and a little later the letters, circulars and magazines that cascaded into the hall. The younger man brought in the milk and collected the newspapers and the mail. He flung the *Telegraph* and the *Independent* on to a chair and leafed through the post.

"Not very interesting," he commented. "A couple of bills, a postcard from Majorca and a billy-doo for the lovely Rosemary."

"Shut up!"

"Oke, boss. Sorry. Anyway, there's nothing important, Mr White. It can all wait till you get back."

Back from where? Presumably from St Xavier's. Greg had no time to ponder the matter. The telephone in the hall had started to ring. But it was scarcely eight o'clock, too early for most people to phone. Greg thought at once of his father, who had recently suffered a stroke.

"Are you expecting a call? You didn't mention it." The older man was suspicious.

"No, but it could be my mother. My father's been ill. You must let me answer it. Bring the phone in here. It's on a long lead. Please!" Greg gritted his teeth.

They did as he asked and, to his relief, the call was for Jean; the woman who organized the rota of voluntary helpers at the local Oxfam shop wanted Jean to replace someone who had a cold. Jean said it was impossible, as Rosemary was sick and couldn't be left.

And the waiting continued. The telephone, the Whites' link with the outside world, remained on the dining-room table, but it only served to mock them. It offered no means of getting help.

3

GREG became conscious that for the last five minutes Rosemary had been fidgeting in her chair, She leant forward over the table, then bent back. She moved her shoulders. She looked about her. Catching what appeared to him a desperate glance from her, Greg, whose wrists were not cuffed, patted her hands and for a moment she clung to one of his fingers.

"Don't touch each other!"

Greg took his hand away. He wondered if Rosemary were trying to tell him something, but he couldn't imagine what. The time was now twenty past eight, still too early for Jean to telephone Rosemary's housemistress to say she was unwell. Perhaps she really was unwell. She was fidgeting more than ever.

"I'm sorry!" she suddenly burst out. "I'm sorry, but I've got to go to the loo — the lavatory."

Greg thought that he could do with

another pee himself, but it was not imperative, and Jean never seemed to have an overpowering need. "For heaven's sake, let her go," he said quietly. "She's not going to run away. You can wait outside the door."

"I'll take her."

Inevitably it was the younger man who had volunteered. Greg saw Rosemary's mouth set and her chin come up, but she didn't protest. She started to make an effort to stand, which proved abortive.

"Oke," the leader said; it was a word of which he and his companion were fond, in spite of their reasonably grammatical speech, and Greg was to remember it. "But no fooling!"

The other man drew Rosemary's chair back from the table. He unlocked the manacles on her ankles and then her wrists, and she spent a minute massaging them before she again tried to stand. She walked uncertainly to the door without a glance at either of her parents, and they heard her begin to mount the stairs.

Rosemary went up a step at a time, pulling herself along by the banisters and half dragging one leg. She hoped she was giving an impression of a cowed girl who was in some pain. This way she planned to take by surprise the revolting smarmy guy following close behind her. She was thankful that he had raised no objection to going upstairs as she had feared he might.

In fact, there was a cloakroom on the ground floor of the house. It was in the hall to one side of the front door, and from the outside looked like a coat cupboard. Rosemary could have gone there more easily but, while it was true that she did want to use the lavatory, she had another purpose which could only be served by the bathroom at the top of the stairs.

For Rosemary had suddenly remembered that the night before, when Tony had brought her home from the birthday party, he had promised to pick her up at eight-thirty the next morning and drive her to school. This meant that in a very few minutes he would be ringing the front doorbell and when no one answered the door he would think it very odd.

She could make a guess at what he

might do. He might try shouting through the letter-box or he might go around to the back of the house and look through the kitchen window. He would wonder why the dining-room curtains were drawn and the light was on; he would surely catch a glimpse of it through the edges of the curtains. So he might bang on the windows — and when there was still no response? He would go home and tell his father. Help would arrive!

That was one conceivable outcome, but Rosemary was a sensible girl and was aware there might be others. Tony might try phoning when he got home, and accept the excuse that she was ill. Or, something she feared much more, if Tony made a nuisance of himself outside the house, the front door might be opened to him and, before he realized what was happening, he could be pulled inside to join them at gunpoint in the dining-room. Somehow she had to warn him and, if it proved at all possible, make him get the police.

By now Rosemary was almost at the top of the stairs. The bathroom, its door ajar, was immediately opposite. She wished the guy behind her was not so close, but she had to take her chance. Without warning she kicked backwards as hard and as viciously as she could. She heard the man grunt with pain, but with a bare foot the blow was less devastating than she had hoped. He dropped his automatic, but managed to save himself from falling by seizing the banister.

Nevertheless, her action gave Rosemary a few precious seconds. She was in the bathroom, the door slammed, the bolt shot, before the man had regained his balance. But she hadn't even unlatched the window, which gave out on to the flat roof of the garage a few feet below, before he was pounding on the door panel and shouting at her.

"Open up, you bitch! Open up!"

Rosemary had no intention of obeying, and he knew it. He stopped his futile shouting and ran at the door, hurling himself shoulder first against it. The door was solid but the bolt was weak. At his third attempt it gave, and he was in the bathroom.

It was not until the banging and shouting started that Greg and Jean, and the man guarding them, realized that some kind of altercation was taking place on the floor above. Instantly they were alert, apprehensive. But they scarcely had time to react before there was the jarring crash of the bathroom door being slammed back against the wall. Moments later Rosemary screamed.

Several things happened simultaneously. The older man, shouting to Greg and Jean to stay where they were, raced from the dining-room. He was back almost immediately to scoop the telephone from the table, just as Jean was stretching out her hands to pull the instrument towards her. Greg, meanwhile, forgetting his cuffed ankles, had leapt to his feet in his desire to go to Rosemary's aid, and after one attempted stride had fallen heavily. As he lay on the floor, entangled in his chair, he could hear the older man calling up the stairs.

"Bring the girl down. Now! At once. Do you hear, Tom? Bring the bloody girl down!"

For a minute there was no response. Rosemary had been halfway out of the bathroom window when the man, whose name she had just learnt was Tom, burst into the room. He had seized her around the waist and pulled her back. As she struggled to resist him they had fallen together to the floor and before she could stop him he had rolled on top of her. He was much bigger and heavier than she was, and she felt that his weight was pressing the breath out of her, but still she struggled.

It was her struggles that aroused him. It was when she felt his hand pulling down her pyjama trousers and forcing her legs apart while the other hand unzipped his fly that she screamed. And then she did the one thing that could have saved her. Instinct made her claw at his face. Chance caused her to grasp his stocking mask. She tugged at it and it came over his head, revealing short sandy hair, blue eyes and the top of what once might have been a broken nose.

The impression she received was fleeting but strong. He had thrust himself away from her, and was staggering to his feet, while at the same time trying to replace his mask. He kicked Rosemary hard, twice, and she cried out.

There was a renewed shout from the stairs. "Come down! Bring the girl! Do you bloody hear me, Tom?"

"Coming!"

This was followed by a stream of abuse that only Rosemary heard; many of the words she didn't even recognize. But she knew that she was safe, at least for the present, and she didn't care when, zipping up his trousers, Tom kicked her again.

"You bitch! You stupid little bitch! Just you wait. I'll get you."

Rosemary ignored the threat. Pulling her pyjamas together and her dressing-gown around her and tying the belt tightly, she stood up. She half expected him to hit her again, but he merely gave her a shove as she edged past him. She walked carefully down the stairs. She had noticed that he was no longer carrying his gun, but knew she had no chance of making a dash for the front door and escaping. The other, older man was standing on the bottom stair, revolver in hand, the telephone tucked under his other arm.

"Come on, girl. Hurry! I don't know

what you've been up to, but you've done no good to yourself or your family." He gestured with his gun to the dining-room door. "Get back in there."

Rosemary ran past him. She hugged her mother first because she was nearer, then went to her father, who had managed to free himself from the chair he had knocked over as he fell, and was standing up. He folded her in his arms and held her to him.

"You're all right?"

"Yes. I tried to get out of the bathroom window but he caught me. He — " She stopped. She had an idea that if she explained more explicitly what had happened it would only cause extra animosity towards her on the part of the man called Tom. She also had an idea that Tom resented his companion's authority since it had in effect interrupted his attempt to — She refused to think about it further.

"Thank God you're all right. I was afraid — "

Greg didn't say what he was afraid of; in his turn, and for different reasons, he didn't dare to put it into words. Over

39

Rosemary's head he exchanged glances with Jean. He knew that she had shared his fear. The last few minutes — only minutes though they had seemed endless — had been hell, not least because he had been incapable of any action, useless, when Rosemary had needed him.

The two men had entered the room close behind Rosemary. The older one banged the telephone down on the table; he was obviously angry.

"Sit down, all of you!" he ordered.

They sat. Without being told, Tom replaced the manacles on Rosemary's wrists and ankles; he was rough, but made no attempt to touch her more than necessary. He had found the gun he had dropped on the stairs, but it was clear that either the incident in the bathroom or fear of his companion had subdued him. He was quiet and sullen.

"What happens now?" Greg demanded. "You are — you're beyond my comprehension. You make no sense. Why won't you say what you want? And then perhaps — How can I know unless you tell me?"

"Mr White, be patient. I'm about to

tell you what we want — what I'm sure you're going to do for us." He shook his head. "If you love your wife and daughter, as clearly you do, you really don't have much choice."

"Suppose you stop these pointless threats and get on with it, then."

"Oke, though there's no hurry. You won't be leaving for about half an hour. Just before nine o'clock, Mr White, you will go out of the house — " He stopped; the front doorbell had rung. "Who'll that be? You said you weren't expecting anyone."

"We're not," Jean said quickly.

"Yes, Mum. Tony. He promised to drive me to school."

"Who's Tony?"

"Tony Pulent. My boyfriend. He lives next door. I forgot he was coming."

"You forgot?" The doorbell pealed again. "Will he go away if no one answers?"

Rosemary shrugged. "I don't know."

"Of course he won't. He's expecting you to be here." The older man pointed towards Greg's ankles. "Undo him," he ordered Tom. "Hurry! Mr White, you're going to answer the door, tell the boy Rosemary's ill and get rid of him. I'll be right beside you, where he can't see me. But I'll be able to see you, and if you make the smallest gesture or speak one wrong word, I'll have this Tony inside the house with the rest of you before you can — "

"I understand." Greg was rubbing his ankles, and he thought how absurd it was that at such a moment he should notice that the chain had made a hole in his sock.

"Come on then! Quick! And, remember, your wife and daughter will be in here."

"How can I forget that?"

Greg tried to smile at them as he obeyed the gesture of the older man's gun to go ahead of him into the hall, but neither Jean nor Rosemary met his gaze. Jean was wondering what she might do if she were in his place, and hoping he wouldn't be rash; Rosemary was torn between worrying about Tony's safety, and wishing Tony would do something heroic that would save them from this present nightmare.

Greg opened the door. "Hello, Tony."

"Hello, Mr White."

Tony straightened himself. He had been bending down to peer through the letter-box and had seen, or thought he had seen, two pairs of trousered legs coming towards him, but now there was only Greg White. Automatically Tony, who had known the Whites all his life and considered their house a second home, made to step into the hall. Greg blocked his way.

Tony was surprised. "I promised I'd pick Rosemary up and drive her to school this morning."

"Yes, so she said, Tony. Unfortunately she's not well."

"Not well?" Tony frowned. "But — "

Tony was nineteen, in his third year at St Xavier's, reading Law. He was, he knew, not the most brilliant of students, but he was working hard and hoped to get a reasonable degree; later, if all went well, he planned to go into politics. As he had a pleasing extrovert personality, plenty of common sense and appeared to like people, there seemed no reason why he shouldn't succeed.

He ran his hand through his thick fair

hair. "Mr White, I don't understand. Rosemary was perfectly well when I dropped her off not many hours ago. What's the matter with her?"

"She running a temperature. I — I don't think it's anything serious. I hope she'll be all right tomorrow."

"Have you sent for the doctor?"

"No, no. I'm sure she doesn't need a doctor."

"Then she can't be too bad. I can come in and have a chat with her, cheer her up. I don't have a lecture till eleven."

"Tony, I'm sorry." Greg was getting more and more conscious of the man with the gun hidden from Tony. He had to get rid of Tony before the man beside him decided to act; it wasn't fair to involve the boy. "Look, she'll call you tomorrow. I promise."

"But, Mr White — I — I don't understand. Is something wrong?"

"No. Everything's fine." Greg forced himself to grin. "Goodbye, Tony. See you."

Greg shut the front door firmly and leant against it. He prayed that Tony would go away and not ring the bell again. "I did my best," he said.

"Sure. You did all right, Mr White, but only just. Another minute and I'd have had that young man in here. Now, back to the dining-room and I'll give you your instructions."

4

"I'VE got rid of Tony. I promised you'd phone him tomorrow, Rosemary." Greg's voice was tight, though he was doing his best to sound normally cheerful.

"Good. I — I'll do that, Dad."

Rosemary wasn't sure whether or not it *was* good. She hadn't wanted Tony dragged into the house, but on the other hand she had been hoping against hope that he could be given a hint that all was not well. He had been their last chance of getting help, and now that seemed to have evaporated. She wondered if she would ever see him again, or if, in spite of their claims, these horrible, revolting men intended to kill them.

"Time for you to phone the school, Mrs White. Early perhaps, but near enough. You know the number?"

Jean nodded. The instrument was pushed across the table to her and she tapped at the keypad. She had

46

considered calling the Pulents instead of the school, or when she got Rosemary's housemistress, who was a sensible woman, saying — what? "Help us! Get the police!" It was unlikely she would have the chance to say more. And how would the men react?

As if reading her thoughts the older man said, "Don't try to be a clever-clever, Mrs White. You'd be sorry. Understood?"

Jean understood. She asked for Miss Westlake and briefly explained to her that Rosemary wouldn't be coming to school because she had a temperature; she hoped it was nothing serious and Rosemary would be there tomorrow. The housemistress was sympathetic, but had no reason to be concerned, and Jean put down the receiver with a small sigh. Like Rosemary, she had been wondering about the extent to which they could depend on their captors' assurance that if they cooperated they would not be harmed. But it was the only hope they had.

The older of the two immediately reinforced that hope. "I'll tell you what we want Mr White to do, what we intend

47

him to do, and I repeat that we won't harm any of you if he agrees to help us. We've got nothing against you. That's on the credit side as far as you're concerned. On the debit side — but Mr White isn't going to let it come to that, are you, Mr White?"

"I don't know."

"You soon will if you refuse, because we're bloody determined to carry out our plan. You'd better believe that. Whatever the cost to us, or to you or your family, Mr White, we're not calling a halt now." The man's voice had become almost hoarse with suppressed passion, which was frightening.

Greg suppressed a shiver. The man might be mad, must be mad, but he had to be believed. There was a steely determination about him, and the phrase 'whatever the cost' was chilling.

"All right. Tell me what you want of me," Greg said quietly. "I may be lacking in imagination but I can't conceive what it may be. What happens if it's impossible — if I can't do it? Have you considered that?"

"You'll be able to do it. It's not in the

least difficult, as long as you follow our instructions exactly."

"Go on," Greg said warily.

"You'll leave this house shortly before nine. You'll take your usual route to the College, down the Banbury Road, and you'll park your car in Broad Street."

"Supposing there isn't a parking space? I often take the bus because parking's so difficult."

"Then you'll just have to park at one or other end of the rows of cars and hope you won't get a ticket. You'll walk fast down Turl Street to the High Street and your College. We've timed it half a dozen times, doing what you'd call research, Mr White, and you should get there shortly before nine-thirty. Anyone you meet that you know you just say 'Morning' but you don't stop for a chat. You go straight to your Master's Lodgings, as you call them, and to this meeting of yours. No funny stuff, you understand. No delays. Timing's of the essence, as they say."

"And I'll be watching you, Mr White," Tom broke in. "Any try at being clever and I'll be popping along to the nearest phone and calling the boss. He'll be right here in your house, waiting, and if I tell him you've double-crossed us, you won't recognize your wife or daughter when you next see them."

Greg clenched his hands so that the nails bit into his palms. He yearned to counter threat with threat, to swear that one day he'd make sure their positions were reversed, and when he had them at his mercy he'd see them in hell. But he knew they'd only laugh at any such outburst. And why not? At this moment any threats he could make were worthless.

"So, to continue, Mr White. You've arrived at your meeting in the Master's study. I take it these meetings start punctually?"

"Yes."

"Good. So it won't have started yet. You sit down, put your briefcase beside you and then excuse yourself. Say you have to go to the toilet, if you like. Instead you leave the Lodgings, return to your car and come home. We'll be watching you, like before, though you may not spot us. If you do just what I've said you'll find your family safe.

Not difficult, is it?"

"No, but — " Greg's face twisted into a grimace. "There's a catch. It's the briefcase. I don't take that with me when I leave the Master's Lodgings, do I?"

"No, Mr White. It stays in the Master's study, beside the chair you sat in, until at exactly twenty-five minutes to ten, when the meeting's well under way, it explodes!"

"Dear God!" whispered Jean.

Greg was shaking his head in disbelief. "You *are* mad! You can't really believe that I'd blow up the Master and — and several of my senior colleagues and wreck part of the College just to please you. Why in hell's name should I?"

"It will please me, yes, but that's not why you'll do it, Mr White. Perhaps you'd be happy to die instead of these colleagues of yours. But what about your wife and daughter? Have you forgotten them? You'll do it for their sake, I'm sure."

"I'm damned if I will. They wouldn't want me to." But Greg spoke without conviction. "Anyway, I don't believe you.

You're bluffing." He felt on stronger ground here. "What would you have to gain?"

"It's what *you've* got to lose you should be thinking about. I said we were determined to carry this out, no matter what the cost to ourselves, or to you, Mr White, and I wasn't joking."

"But why? Why?"

"That's our business. It doesn't concern you. All that concerns you is doing what you've been told."

"And if I refuse?"

"Mr White, do I have to repeat everything? You're supposed to be a clever man. Sure, you can refuse, but then you'll take the consequences, you and your family. The one thing I'm not doing is bluffing."

"He means it, Dad." Rosemary was frightened.

"Greg, she's right. He *does* mean it," Jean repeated. "For God's sake consider what he's saying."

"But there would be no point. If I refuse his plan's failed. Don't you realize that? It would be stupid to hurt any of us. The police won't bother overmuch about — about what's happened so far, but if — "

"Mr White, if you refuse — and I don't think you will once you've considered the matter — we'll have to find another don who can be persuaded to help us — and try again." He held up his hand to stop Greg's reply. "I know what you're going to say, but you're wrong. You won't have warned the police about our plan, because when we go away from here, we'll have left you cuffed and helpless with the briefcase just out of your reach. You won't be telling anyone anything."

There was a gasp of horror from Jean. "Greg — "

"You murderous swine!" he cried, and choked.

This was a nightmare. He stared at the two men. The fact that they were dressed from head to foot in black made them ludicrously unreal. They were like characters from a bad melodrama. They didn't behave consistently; sometimes they didn't even seem sure of their lines. Cups of tea, and toast, closely followed by unspeakable threats of violence. And why me, he thought, why did they pick on me? He was unaware that he had spoken aloud.

"Do you wish we'd picked on someone else, Mr White? Would you rather be in your Master's study at nine thirty-five this morning when the briefcase explodes, or on your way home to your wife and daughter?"

Greg didn't answer. He had been tempted to say, yes, he would rather be in the Master's study, ignorant of what was to happen — and innocent of anyone's death. But that choice wasn't his. It had been made for him, and he'd been lumbered with a far more difficult, indeed an impossible choice between Rosemary and Jean on the one hand, and several people, most of whom he liked and respected, on the other. But . . . He put his elbows on the table and buried his face in his hands.

"I'll give you five minutes to decide, Mr White. That's all we can spare. But don't hope we'll change our minds. If you refuse to help us you'll die at nine thirty-five, all three of you."

"And I might have a bit of fun first." The younger man, leaning in the doorway, laughed suddenly. "I quite fancy your daughter, Mr White."

"No!" Rosemary cried immediately. "No, not that! Dad, please don't let him."

"You can't, Greg. For God's sake! I'd take their damned bomb myself if I could, rather than — Rosemary's a child, your child, with her whole life in front of her. You can't believe the Master and a lot of old men are more important than she is. Don't you love her?" Jean was incensed.

"They're not all old men," Greg said absently. "They're mostly around my age and married, with their own wives and children." He sighed. "And of course I love our daughter. Rosemary, you know that, don't you, darling?"

"Yes, Dad, I know that, but — " She shivered. "I can't bear the idea of that — that guy — "

"No. I can understand that." Greg was bitter. He squared his shoulders. "All right. They win. I'll take this blasted bomb. I'll blow up the Master's Lodgings. I'll kill a few of my colleagues. And God forgive me!"

"Would you prefer God to forgive you for letting your daughter be raped and all of us murdered?" Jean's voice was harsh, showing the strain she was under.

"No," Greg said. He felt numb. He had made his decision and he would stick with it. He had no choice. In fact, he thought, the decision hadn't been his. Jean and Rosemary had made it for him. Jean had hardly understood that there was a decision to be made. To her his hesitation had been a kind of betrayal. "When do I go?" he asked dully.

"Right now!" There was relief as well as satisfaction in the older man's voice. "Two minutes for my mate to get going, then I'll be watching you leave, Mr White. Remember he'll be following you all the way."

"I'll remember." Greg pushed back in his chair; his ankles were still manacled. "I'll need to walk," he said.

"Natch." The younger man, Tom, thrust himself off the doorframe against which he was leaning. He dived under the table and freed Greg's legs. Then he tossed the key to his companion. "I'll be off." He gave the Whites an exaggerated salute.

"Put the phone back in the hall as you go."

"Oke. Be seeing you, Rosemary dear." He blew her a kiss as he went.

Greg stood up. He leant both hands on the table and addressed the remaining man. "I'm doing what you want," he said, "but I swear to you that if that yobbo ever comes near my daughter once this is all over, I'll kill him."

"He won't, Mr White. He won't. You'll never see or hear from either of us again. Just deliver the briefcase and return to your family. Then you can forget about this little lot."

Greg didn't bother to contradict him. He knew he would never forget the two men, or the horror they had brought with them. And it wasn't over yet. "Where is the bloody briefcase?"

"In the hall, by the front door. Treat it with care. Put it on the seat beside you while you're driving." He got to his feet. The revolver was steady in his hand. "Come on now. I'll see you out."

Greg gave Rosemary a quick hug and

leant across her to kiss Jean, who offered him her cheek. None of them spoke. There was nothing to be said. Rosemary was near tears.

★ ★ ★

Jean twisted in her seat so that, moving her cuffed wrists, she could entwine her fingers with Rosemary's. She felt the girl start as the front door slammed.

"Dad's gone," Rosemary whispered.

"Yes. Don't worry, darling. Everything will be all right. He won't let us down."

"No, but — Such a lot can go wrong. He could easily be delayed. Another car could run into him or he could knock down a pedestrian or — or — "

Or he could try to do something clever, and fail, Jean thought, but she didn't voice the notion. She didn't trust Greg over this. In his place she wouldn't have hesitated; surely the family had to take precedence over half a dozen academics, some of whom he didn't particularly like. True, they had wives and children too, but in the circumstances his own family should come first.

"And these men, Mum? They said the explosion's going to happen at nine thirty-five, but are they sure? I suppose they made this bomb themselves. How expert are they? Bombs don't always go off when they're meant to and — and I'm afraid for Dad."

"So am I, Rosemary."

It wasn't a lie. She *was* afraid for Greg, but she was more afraid for Rosemary and herself. Rosemary was right. Even if Greg didn't attempt some silly heroic act, the bomb might go off at the wrong time and in the wrong place — and what would the gunman do then? When he learnt that they had failed to achieve their purpose would he shoot the pair of them out of pure vindictiveness?

He had returned to the dining-room, and it was clear to them that he was feeling the strain as much as they were, for he paced up and down in front of them and glanced at his watch every few seconds. Once Jean asked him the time, but he didn't answer.

Nevertheless the minutes had to be passing, however slowly — and still the phone didn't ring. They had to assume that Greg was carrying out his task as ordered and that nothing had interfered with him. Jean began to hope that after all the worst wasn't going to happen; she refused to think about the Master and the others who might be killed or maimed with him.

Then suddenly their captor stopped his pacing. He swung round and levelled his gun at the pair of them. Rosemary gasped.

"Has — has the bomb exploded?" Jean asked quickly. "We wouldn't have heard it from here, would we? But no one's phoned."

"It's only twenty minutes past nine. Your husband ought to have parked his car by now and started to walk down Turl Street, so I'll say goodbye. I'm off."

"You're leaving? Now! You mean you'll kill us although Greg's doing what you want? But you said — you promised — we'd come to no harm if — "

"Mrs White, I know what I said. There's no need to remind me. I'm not going to hurt you, so you don't have to worry. Just you wait there as you are till your husband or someone else arrives. I'll put the keys to your cuffs in the lounge."

Jean bit her tongue. She had nearly said thank-you, but to thank a criminal who had physically and mentally abused them because he was kind enough to spare their lives would have been absurd — or was she falling for the so-called Stockholm syndrome? Nevertheless, in her relief, she had difficulty in stemming the tide of gratitude she felt.

"All right."

"Only one thing. When the police question you, as they will, you can't describe me or my mate. You don't remember a thing about us. And that goes for Mr White too. Understood?"

"We couldn't describe you if we wanted to." Jean spoke with conviction; she didn't notice that beside her Rosemary had suddenly tensed.

"Oke. Then I'll be off."

They didn't answer, but they listened. They heard him go into the sitting-room. From there he went to the kitchen, and they waited. It seemed a long wait, and certainly he didn't leave the house immediately. But after two or three minutes the side door slammed.

Jean released her breath, "Rosemary, I think — I think we're safe."

"I hope so. But — but what about Dad? What's happened to him?"

5

AS soon as he emerged from the dining-room Greg had seen the briefcase standing, handle upright, on the floor of the hall. It was very like his own. He gritted his teeth. The next hour was going to be a period of terrible stress and anxiety, and he told himself that he must forget Jean and Rosemary, and forget the consequences of his imposed mission. It was essential to concentrate on carrying out the task accurately and without arousing the least suspicion on the part of Tom and any other watcher whom the pair of gunmen might have stationed outside.

His car, a red Ford Fiesta, five years old, was parked in the short driveway in front of the garage which housed their new Rover. He placed the briefcase carefully on the gravel, unlocked the front left-hand door of the Ford, placed the briefcase carefully on the seat and relocked the door before going around the car and getting behind the wheel. He wondered if he should try to wedge the case upright, but he had nothing with which to do this.

His hand was unsteady, but his second attempt to insert the ignition key in its place was successful. He started the engine and backed the car into the road, wincing as it bumped over the gutter. Some fifty yards behind him a plain white van drew away from the kerb, and further back he saw a motorcyclist wearing a yellow crash helmet, but otherwise dressed in black. Either or both of these could have been the escort he had been promised.

He drove the length of the street. A neighbour, busy working in her front garden, waved to him and he waved back. A party of schoolboys, laughing and jostling each other, strayed off the pavement and he gave them a warning hoot. There was a normality about the scene that was reassuring. Even the slight smell of the fruit drops which Rosemary liked to suck and which had permeated the Ford over the years was comforting. But there was no way he could forget the briefcase on the seat beside him, and the enormity of what he had to do appalled him.

He stopped at the corner on to the Banbury Road, and waited for a gap in the southbound traffic. To his dismay he noticed on of his students standing at the bus stop nearby. And Jack Graham had seen him! Greg swore. He could not possibly have Jack in the car. He knew nothing about the bomb except that it was due to go off at nine thirty-five and he had been told to treat the briefcase with care. He had no idea how volatile the damned thing might be. For all he knew it might explode at any moment, and he couldn't risk an unnecessary life. In any case, any attempt to stop for a hitch-hiker might well trigger a tragedy at his home.

So, staring straight ahead of him, Greg turned the corner and drove past the bus stop. As he went by he caught a glimpse of Jack Graham's face, and in other circumstances the change of expression from grateful anticipation to stunned disbelief would have made him laugh. But he was in no laughing mood.

The incident had brought home to him the fact that he was a menace to anyone near him — the occupants of a passing car, a pedestrian waiting to cross the street, a cyclist delayed beside him at a red light.

The man in black gear with a yellow helmet whom he had seen when leaving his house had overtaken him, and was disappearing into the distance on his motorbike, but the white van was still behind him. He wondered if he had any option but to drive to the centre of the city and go to his College. If he had thought earlier he might have driven to Parks and abandoned the car with its deadly burden in an open space where an explosion would destroy grass, trees and flowerbeds but, with luck, not a single human being. But then again, what would have happened to Rosemary and Jean?

Anyway, it was too late now. He was heading for the most populated area of Oxford. Even as he accepted this frightening fact and what it might mean, he saw a traffic warden step into the road and hold up a warning hand. He braked sharply, too sharply. The briefcase started to fall forward but, thrusting an arm sideways, he just managed to save it.

His car stopped on the edge of a pedestrian crossing and the traffic warden glared angrily at him. A woman wheeling a double pushchair of the kind made for twins began to walk across the road. To Greg she moved with agonizing slowness. A taxi with an elderly couple in the back drew up beside him. A motorbike suddenly appeared in the narrow space between his car and the taxi. Behind Greg was a bus, and on the opposite side of the road were several stationary vehicles heading north. Two women were standing on the pavement close beside him, chatting.

Greg shut his eyes. No, he prayed, not now! If the bomb exploded — He refused to contemplate the horror that would ensue. But, after all, if it did happen he would know nothing about it; that was the only consolation.

There was a loud hooting behind him. The traffic warden stepped forward and banged on his windscreen. Greg opened his eyes and swallowed hard. The woman with the twins had reached the opposite pavement. The traffic, except for the lane he was blocking, was once more flowing freely.

Hurriedly Greg got into gear and drove off. He reached the lights in St Giles'. They showed red and he prepared to stop again. He was beginning to worry about the time. If he were late reaching the College . . . He looked in his rear-view mirror. The white van had overtaken the bus and was still behind him. But the lights had changed and thankfully he accelerated away.

He turned into the Broad. As he had expected, there was a solid double line of cars parked in the centre of the wide road, and no space was available. Then a Mini started to pull out. Greg drew up and waited. The woman at the wheel of the Mini was not the most efficient of drivers and seemed to have difficulty in reversing. Greg hooted impatiently and she waved an apologetic hand as she drove off. Greg ignored the friendly gesture.

He parked quickly. Broad Street is entitled to its name, and it occurred to him that if he merely abandoned the briefcase in his car here the bomb might explode without harming anyone and with the minimum of devastation. But of course he couldn't think of such a solution. He was still being watched. The white van was parked outside Balliol. Even if he went and accosted the driver, whom he assumed to be Tom, he couldn't depend on holding him until the police came and, if Tom got away, what might happen to Jean and Rosemary? Once more he was faced with the same dreadful dilemma.

He wiped his face and hands on his handkerchief. He was sweating badly and he knew he had to hurry. Time was passing. If he sat there much longer he would be blown to pieces and the likelihood was that he wouldn't have saved Jean and Rosemary. He got out and went round the Ford, opened the passenger door and gingerly picked up the briefcase. He crossed the road and started to walk down the Turl.

He moved at a brisk pace, wishing there were not so many people about. As he passed Exeter College a student dashed out of the lodge. He knocked heavily against Greg and in a vain effort to save the pile of books he was carrying nearly wrenched the briefcase from Greg's grasp.

"Sorry, sir!"

"You — "

Greg bit back the expletives. He leant against the wall of the College and hugged the briefcase to his chest. For a split second he thought he was about to collapse.

The student, already on his knees collecting his books, looked up at him curiously. "Are you all right, sir? I'm awfully sorry."

Greg nodded. He pushed himself away from the wall and continued down the Turl, carefully shielding the briefcase from passers-by. In his anxiety he had lost all sense of time, and even forgotten that he was wearing his watch. Now he remembered, and glanced at it. It had seemed to him an age since he left home, and he was both surprised and relieved to see that he had over five minutes in hand *if* — *if* the bloody thing had been timed accurately.

But now he was committed. Whatever wild ideas he might have had before, there was no longer any alternative. He was taking the briefcase and its unholy contents to St Xavier's. This way he could at least expect with some confidence to save Rosemary and Jean, and everyone other than those for whom the bomb had been intended. He lengthened his stride, not bothering to look back to see if he could spot a follower; there were too many people about to make this feasible.

"Greg, my dear chap, just the man I want a word with."

Even in ordinary circumstances Greg wouldn't have welcomed the intervention. The man standing squarely in front of him and blocking his way was the acknowledged bore of St Xavier's Senior Common Room. He was a massive character whose habit was to get someone in a corner to have 'a word' and then keep his unfortunate victim there for half an hour. He was the last person Greg wanted to meet.

"Sorry, Christopher, I haven't time at the moment."

"It will only take two ticks. It's about one of your students, young Morrison. He has rooms above me on 'C' Staircase and — "

"Complain to the Bursar!"

Greg dodged into the road, circumventing the large bulk that was obstructing him, ignoring the man's surprise at his brusque rudeness and causing a passing cyclist to fall off his machine. He hurried on, oblivious of the angry cries behind him, reached the High Street and dived into the porter's lodge of St Xavier's College.

St Xavier's was a relatively new College. It was not large, and by modern Oxford standards rather exclusive. Built on the corner of the Turl and the High, it occupied the sites of what had once been the Mitre Hotel and some of the eclectic shops behind it. It consisted of three quadrangles. The Master's Lodgings were in the first quad to the right of the porter's lodge and, though an integral part of the College, constituted in effect a small, self-contained house.

Greg returned the porters' greetings and walked rapidly across the quad to the Lodgings. In these days of security consciousness a stranger might have been asked to state his business and open his briefcase, but no one would have thought to question a Fellow as well known as Greg White.

He went up the two steps to the heavy oak door, which was already unlocked in preparation for the meeting that was about to take place. He entered the short, square-shaped hall in time to see the Bursar go into the Master's study. He could hear a murmur of voices and guessed he was among the last arrivals. Then Ailsa Mackay came out of her office.

Ailsa was the Master's secretary. She was a plain, shy woman, one of Greg's first pupils, and she had been expected to get an excellent degree. But her father had died, there had been family difficulties, and she had gone down at the end of her second year. Subsequently she had returned to Oxford to take a secretarial course, and Greg had been influential in her getting her present post. If she carried a torch for him, she never let it show. They were friends, no more.

But Greg liked her, admired her, and was sorry for her, though he wouldn't have admitted the last. He had also completely forgotten about her. Her sudden appearance, a sheaf of papers in her hand, made him realize that she, who had never had the best of luck, would be sitting in the Master's study taking shorthand notes when the bomb he was carrying exploded. Faced with such a potential — and totally innocent — victim of the act he was about to commit he knew at last that he couldn't go through with it.

"Greg, are you all right? You've gone awfully pale."

"Yes. Yes. I'm all right."

He had to think and he had to think quickly. There was very little time left. What could he do with the bloody briefcase? He could not take it into the study, but he could not leave the Lodgings and the College with it still in his hand. He must put it somewhere — the lavatory? — and then walk out of the College, showing himself to the watching Tom as empty-handed, and set off up the Turl to his car — and home, to Jean and Rosemary.

"Greg, what is it? Something's wrong. Tell me! I'll help if I possibly can."

"It's nothing!" She was holding his arm and he pulled it away, being careful not to jog the briefcase. "Tummy upset, that's all. Must go to the loo."

Conscious of Ailsa gazing after him, Greg strode towards the cloakroom which was off the hall. He was wondering about the best place to put the briefcase. He thought of the cistern but that wasn't big enough. In the end he managed to find room for it behind the lavatory pan. He activated the flush and left. He could only hope that no one would go in there for the next few minutes, and that two thick walls would provide some protection for those in the study across the hall.

Thankful that Ailsa hadn't waited for him to emerge he let himself out of the Lodgings. There were several people in the quad, among them Tony Pulent, who was leaning against the wall of the Lodgings chatting to Hugh Fremont and a younger man whom Greg didn't recognize. It was impossible to ignore them.

"Hello, Greg. I was hoping to see you. I'm just here for the day. Let me introduce my kid brother, Richard."

"Hugh — " Greg began.

Hugh Fremont was one of the most brilliant students that St Xavier's had produced. He had gone down a year ago and was at present a Third Secretary at the Foreign Office; great things were expected of him.

"How do you do, sir."

Richard Fremont held out his hand and Greg, shaking it briefly, was made aware of the dampness of his own palm. He couldn't stop. There was no time. But he couldn't leave the trio where they were; they were much too close to the wall of the cloakroom for safety, and any second now —

Tony, who knew him best, was regarding him anxiously. "Mr White, are you unwell?"

"Listen!" Greg snapped. "Do as I say and don't ask questions. Go to my rooms — all three of you! Now! At once!"

Without waiting to witness their amazed

reactions, Greg sprinted across the quad to the lodge. As he reached it he caught a glimpse over his shoulder of the three young men moving slowly, very slowly, away from the vicinity of the Lodgings in the direction of his staircase. He wanted to scream at them to hurry, but he had to save his breath. To impress Dobson, the head porter, with the need for action was the more immediate necessity.

He burst into the lodge, and forced himself to speak emphatically and authoritatively, but without panic. "Dobson, this is an emergency! There's a bomb in a briefcase in the cloakroom of the Master's Lodgings. It's due to go off any moment. Clear the Lodgings! Phone the police! You know what to do."

Dobson had been a sergeant-major before he was invalided out of the army. He was used to emergencies and to taking and giving orders. Greg had scarcely finished speaking before he was shouting at the junior porter, a youth called Fairchild, who was open-mouthed at what he had just heard, to 'get over there and get everyone out'. At the same time, Dobson himself was dialling 999.

Greg didn't wait. He had done all he could. Now he must make sure of Jean's and Rosemary's safety. He paused for a moment outside the College. The High Street was busy with cars and bicycles, its pavements thronged with pedestrians. But there was no sign of a white van and, if the watchful Tom was on foot, Greg had no means of identifying him. Quickly Greg set off for his car, and home.

6

THE bomb exploded exactly on time just after Greg had turned the corner into Turl Street. The dull boom was loud and clear, and Greg even thought that he could feel the pavement shake for a moment beneath his feet. He realized at once that his warning had been too late. There was no hope that everyone had been able to comprehend a warning, appreciate the need for immediate action and leave the Master's Lodgings. Indeed, there was every possibility that the meeting had just started and they would all be in the study. All? Suddenly he remembered Lady Pinel and the cook-housekeeper; until that moment he had completely forgotten about them.

Feeling physically sick, he ignored the surge of excitement that surrounded him. Pedestrians stopped dead, and so did the traffic, brought to a halt at the corner of the High. Drivers left their vehicles.

Everywhere startled faces expressed anxiety, curiosity, apprehension.

But almost immediately some individuals, mostly men, realizing the significance of the sound, began to run towards its source. Others shrugged and continued on their way. Greg himself hesitated, then decided to join the latter group. Questions would undoubtedly follow him, sooner rather than later he imagined, but his first priority was the welfare of his family. For the moment he must forget the consequences of his enforced action.

★ ★ ★

When the bomb went off, Fairchild, unaware that the main door of the Master's Lodgings was unlocked, had rung the bell and was pounding on the brass knocker. His senior, Dobson, had left the lodge and was running towards him, repeating his instructions to go in and get everyone out. Tony Pulent and the two Fremont brothers had reached the middle of the quad, and there were perhaps half a dozen other dons or graduate students or undergraduates in the vicinity. All were startled, but none appreciated the immediate significance of what had happened.

One undergraduate who was leaning out of his window on the far side of the quad talking to a friend below, had an excellent view of events. Later, he described them graphically. "There was a sound like an enormous muted bang," he said. "The shock came up through the floor. Part of the front wall of the Lodgings bulged outwards and then seemed to disintegrate. Stone and rubble showered down, overwhelming poor Fairchild. The blast knocked Dobson to the ground, but even as the dust settled he was staggering to his feet. The door to the Lodgings had been blown out and the chaos inside the hall was visible. It was horrific."

* * *

Inside the Lodgings the meeting in the Master's study had just started. It was late, three minutes late, the amount of grace the Master had allowed Greg when

Ailsa Mackay had said that Mr White had gone to the cloakroom and must be coming any moment. Sir Philip Pinel, as everyone in the College knew, was a stickler for punctuality and was not prepared to wait until — to use his own words — "Mr White condescended to grace us with his presence".

It was ironic that the Master should have made such an acid remark about a man who, by his quick thinking and his actions, had almost certainly saved his life and the lives of the Bursar, three senior dons and Ailsa Mackay. For there was no doubt, according to the subsequent report of the police bomb squad, that had the explosion taken place in the study it was highly unlikely that anyone in the room would have survived.

As it was, though the study wall giving on to the hall stood up to the blast, the door was flung open and a small tornado engulfed the room. The window shattered, throwing glass splinters everywhere. Pictures fell to the floor, small objects, some of them surprisingly heavy, flew through the air like missiles, inflicting damage to people and property. Dust made breathing difficult and, as it settled, there became visible a nightmarish scene.

The Master lay slumped in his chair, blood streaming into his eyes from a cut in his brow inflicted by a heavy glass ashtray. The Bursar, who had chronic asthma, was gasping for breath. Ailsa had been hit in the face by a silver cigarette box and was badly bruised, her nose bleeding. Dr Harold Dawson, Senior Tutor of the College, seemed to be unconscious, though the reason was not immediately apparent. All those in the study were covered with small splinters of glass from the shattered window and all were suffering from shock. The room itself was a shambles.

Then, as the noise and dust subsided, from the hall came a high-pitched wailing scream that went on endlessly.

It was audible in the quad outside. It galvanized Hugh Fremont who, followed by his brother and Tony, raced towards the Lodgings. Dobson was already pulling at the rubble with his bare hands in an attempt to free young Fairchild. Hugh

Fremont ignored him; others, recovering from their initial surprise and horror, were coming to help. Hugh led the way into the Lodgings.

The source of the screaming soon became clear. It was Lady Pinel, the Master's wife. She had been in her bedroom, dressing to go out, at the time the bomb exploded, and she had started to run downstairs, only to find that the last half-dozen steps were missing and that the hall was in a state of devastation. Stunned, she had retreated up the stairs and sat down, screaming hysterically.

"Give me a leg up," Hugh ordered his brother.

"It may collapse," Richard pointed out quickly.

But he did as he was told and Hugh, having tested the banister at the height of his reach, managed with a heave from Richard to pull himself on to the stairs. He crawled gingerly towards Lady Pinel, whose screams continued until he slapped her across the face, once, twice. He admitted afterwards to Greg that it had given him a good deal of satisfaction. Beatrice Pinel was not one of his favourite women.

Luckily, however, she was tall and thin and he was able to lower her down to Richard, who took her out into the quad and sat her on the grass, where she received help from a woman student who seemed to know what to do. Meanwhile, the Bursar had of his own accord staggered outside and was gasping and choking as he struggled for breath. The two dons who had suffered least, Dr Desmond Ansley and Mr Brian Mead, were doing their best to carry the Master from the Lodgings. Tony led Ailsa to safety and others carried out the unconscious Harold Dawson. Hugh, who had been forced to jump down from the staircase and had twisted his ankle, limped after them. In a matter of minutes the Lodgings had been cleared.

No one had been killed. Indeed, it seemed at the time that no one was to suffer permanent injury as a result of the outrage, though Dawson, an elderly man, had a minor heart attack and Fairchild was to spend some weeks in hospital with concussion and a broken leg. The remaining injuries were comparatively slight. Nevertheless, it had been an appalling incident, and a large part of the ground floor of the Master's Lodgings had been wrecked.

When the authorities arrived — first, two police officers from a patrol car, closely followed after a radio call by police reinforcements, ambulances, the fire service, and a little later senior police officers and the Thames Valley police bomb squad — the front quad of St Xavier's resembled the aftermath of an air raid combined with a battlefield casualty clearing station.

The fire service was not needed, but the ambulances were, and the more seriously injured were soon on their way to hospital. As soon as it was realized that the cause of the incident was almost certainly a bomb of some kind, the police started to clear the whole area — the College itself, the neighbouring buildings and the High Street, where a crowd of sightseers had gathered; some had even come into the College quad itself to gawp at the results of the explosion. They went without argument, aware now of the danger to themselves if there should be a second explosion — women with shopping-bags, a party of foreign visitors, some undergraduates. The only person who gave trouble was the Pinels' cook-housekeeper, who had been on a shopping excursion to the covered market nearby. She protested strongly at not being allowed to enter the College and only permitted to leave her heavy basket in the porter's lodge after it had been searched.

★ ★ ★

Among those who had managed to view the scene inside the quad was a young man, fairly tall, thin, with sandy hair, blue eyes and a crooked nose. He was wearing black trousers and a green leather jacket over a black shirt. There was nothing unusual about him — except perhaps for an ill-concealed grin — and he made no impression on the police officers. This was a pity, for Tom had left his white van in Broad Street, followed Greg to St Xavier's, seen him emerge without the briefcase, and noted with satisfaction the time of the explosion.

7

IT was at least fifteen minutes before the Thames Valley Police control room at their Kidlington Headquarters fully appreciated the situation. A bomb at St Xavier's College? Part of the Master's Lodgings destroyed? A number of casualties? Sure, there had been bombs in other parts of the area covered by the Thames Valley Police — one such incident near Reading was even now under investigation — but never before in the very centre of Oxford City. The idea was, at first, unthinkable.

But training and reason reasserted themselves and the Inspector on duty alerted Sir Philip Midvale, the Chief Constable, who was immediately faced with a dilemma. Normally, outrages of this kind would not be treated as ordinary crimes, and the inquiries — demanding, as they usually did, coordination and cooperation with technical personnel, specialized forensic experts and even the Special Branch from the Met. — would be handled by a specialist officer and his team. But the officer in question was already in Reading, and there was nothing for it but to hand the matter over to the Serious Crime Squad. Fortunately, he reflected quickly, Tansey was available.

Detective Chief Inspector Richard Tansey was far from being a stupid man and, now in his late-thirties, he had few illusions about human nature and would have claimed that nothing could surprise him. But he was surprised now, when he answered the Chief Constable's urgent call.

His first reaction mirrored that of the Inspector in the control room. The area covered by the Thames Valley Police was not without its quota of crime. There were the usual numbers of burglaries, murders, rapes, acts of violence and less serious offences every year, not least in Oxford City itself. This, however, was the first occasion that had seen wanton destruction — and destruction apparently caused by a bomb, of all things — inflicted on the persons and property of a College and, what was more, apparently within the College.

"Get along there at once, Chief Inspector, and take overall charge. You'll find a uniformed Inspector called Carey holding the fort and doing what he can till you arrive. The bomb squad technical boys are also on the job." There had been an edge to the Chief Constable's voice as he was briefing Tansey — a minimal briefing, for few details were available at that point. "Until we know more, you'll report direct to me."

"Yes, sir." Tansey thought with regret of the pile of files remaining in his in-tray. "You say there was a warning?"

"Apparently. Given by one of the dons, according to the head porter who called us originally. But it was much too late. Now, as I say, the bomb squad's already there, and they'll tell you what they require, if anything. I imagine the first thing will be a preliminary search for another device, if that's not been started already, and then a fingertip search of the immediate area — but the bomb boys will probably do that themselves; they know what to look for better than we do. Anyway, you know you can count on my full support."

"Thank you, sir."

Tansey had no need to ask why the Chief Constable was taking such a personal interest in this case. First, there was its seemingly unique character and, secondly, Tansey knew that Philip Midvale had himself been up at Oxford, and was attached to his old university.

"We must find the villains, Chief Inspector, and quickly."

"I'll do my best, sir," replied Tansey a little doubtfully. He knew that such inquiries sometimes stretched over long periods, even years, before anyone was brought to justice.

"I'm sure you will." Midvale heaved his large bulk out of his outsize chair, signifying not only that the interview was at an end, but that he was unusually tense. His comment matched Tansey's private thoughts. "Though I've got an idea this may not be all that elementary a case." He gave Tansey a wry smile.

The remark and the smile brought an answering grin from the Chief Inspector. Tansey liked his Chief Constable and over the years had developed a close relationship with him. He also had an immense respect for his superior's judgement and instinct. But he hoped that on this occasion, their instincts had let down both Midvale and himself, and it would prove a simple case, — preferably, for example, an attempt at vandalism that had somehow got out of hand.

Tansey returned to his own office and acted rapidly. He sent for Detective-Sergeant Abbot, whom he planned to take with him. Bill Abbot was a cheerful, extrovert type, born and bred in Oxfordshire, and his knowledge of local people had often proved useful in the past. Tansey was aware that the explosion at St Xavier's probably had no local connections, but Abbot was always an excellent support. And since the Chief Constable had given him a free hand, Tansey decided to include a woman in his team. He chose a uniformed officer, WPC Robertson who, though young, was a plump and motherly type, but extremely shrewd. He knew that St Xavier's had begun to admit women undergraduates some years ago, and thought that Robertson might prove useful.

Tansey briefed Abbot and Robertson as well as he could, and they set off. It was a straight run from the Headquarters of the Thames Valley Force in Kidlington to the centre of Oxford, and Abbot drove fast. Yet by the time they arrived they found that some order had been restored in place of the initial chaos.

They were met by Inspector Carey who, with the help of the Bursar, had been busy setting up an incident room and an interview room. At least the College had plenty of space for such activities, and the Bursar — his name was Peter Lacque — was an efficient character who would probably have risen to the very top of the business world had he not been plagued with asthma all his life. In the present crisis, once he had regained his ability to breathe normally, he had assumed control of St Xavier's and was proving his worth.

Tansey introduced himself and the two officers with him, and Carey started his briefing without being asked. First and most importantly, the College had been subjected to a preliminary search for further devices, and at least the front quad declared safe. The end of Turl Street and part of the High Street had been cordoned off for the present. In response to Tansey's inquiry about casualties, Carey said that ambulances had taken the Master and Lady Pinel, and a Dr Harold Dawson and the young porter, Fairchild, to hospital. A woman secretary, Ailsa Mackay, though bruised and bloodstained, the side of her face swollen and discoloured, had accepted first aid, but refused to go to hospital. Dobson had returned to his lodge, and had also obstinately refused to budge from his place of duty.

As a first step Tansey instructed WPC Robertson to obtain from the Bursar and Dobson a complete list of members of St Xavier's, from the Master to the most lowly undergraduate, with the position that each individual held. He also wanted a list of all the employees and staff who helped to keep the College running. And, in particular, he needed to know who had been seen near the scene of the crime before, during and after the explosion.

They had all been evacuated, of course, and Robertson was to try to discover their present whereabouts.

Next the Chief Inspector went with Abbot to the Master's Lodgings, where it was obvious that a detailed so-called 'fingertip' search of every square inch of the ground floor and the area outside the building was already in progress. The head of the bomb squad, a quiet, bespectacled young man, came out to meet them.

"Quite a mess, sir," he said, by way of a greeting. "But it could have been much worse. Whoever planted the device put it in a damned stupid place — from his point of view, I mean. It was in the downstairs cloakroom, jammed behind the toilet pan, and the pan partially shielded the rest of the house. Even so, it was a powerful little trinket. It was lucky no one was killed."

"I'd like to see inside."

"Of course, sir. There's no danger. I expect Inspector Carey's told you that this quad has been declared safe, and I'm practically certain there isn't another bomb elsewhere in the College.

Incidentally, from the debris we've found already, I'd guess that this one was in a leather bag of some kind."

Tansey and Abbot followed him into the building. Two men were still examining the cloakroom. One of them said, "I've found a bit of a timing device. It looks pretty primitive to me."

"What about the bomb itself?" asked Tansey. "It's done an impressive amount of damage, I would say, but could it have been someone's idea of a black joke that misfired?"

The three experts shook their heads in unison. "Definitely not," said the senior man. "We shan't be certain what explosive was used until we get everything we find back to the lab, but I can tell you now that this was no prank. It was for real, all right. Whoever planted the thing must have had a fair idea of the impact it would have. On the other hand . . ."

"Yes?" Tansey prompted.

"It's early days yet. I don't want to stick my neck out. But somehow this hasn't got the hallmarks of a professional job. For one thing, if it was an act of pure terrorism, why choose a small and not particularly well-known College? Why not Balliol or Christ Church?" He grinned suddenly. "I'm afraid I'm usurping your territory, Chief Inspector."

Tansey laughed. "I'm always open to suggestions. If you have any more, add them at the end of your report."

"Will do, sir."

Tansey and Abbot picked their way through the rubble of the hall, had a look at the truncated staircase and then inspected the Master's study. The rest of the ground floor, except for the odd picture that had fallen off a wall, appeared largely undamaged.

"What next, sir?" asked Abbot as they emerged into the quad. "The Bursar?"

"Not yet. We'll give him a little more time to help Inspector Carey and settle us in. We may be here for some while." Tansey was already striding towards the porter's lodge.

"Let's have a chat with this chap Dobson. It was he who gave the warning, late though it was."

★ ★ ★

In the lodge Ailsa Mackay had been disinfecting the cuts on Dobson's hands and, in spite of his protests, putting dressings on the worst of them. She had borrowed a white coat from a science student to cover the bloodstains on her blouse and skirt, but she couldn't disguise her swollen face. Nor was her appearance improved by her worried frown at the trend of her talk with Dobson.

"I don't understand, Miss Mackay," Dobson reiterated. "If Mr White knew there was a bomb in the Lodgings — "

"I don't understand either, Dobson, but I'm sure Mr White will have a perfectly good explanation."

"What about the police? What shall I tell them?"

Ailsa sighed. "The truth. Answer their questions. But — but there's no need to volunteer information, Dobson."

The porter laughed. "I learnt that long ago in the army, Miss Mackay."

The arrival of Tansey and Abbot prevented further private conversation. Ailsa gave her name, hurriedly excused herself and then made her escape, although she knew that she was probably only securing a temporary respite. Tansey made no attempt to detain her, but he thought her eagerness to depart interesting.

"William Dobson, sir. At your service."

"Thank you, Mr Dobson. I was sure the police could depend on your help, which is why we came here to start our inquiries, once we'd surveyed the scene." Tansey wondered why he was being so unctuous, and realized that he had been copying the porter; neither of them was entirely sincere. "It was you who gave the alarm, wasn't it?"

"You could say that, sir."

"And just what could *you* say, Dobson?" Tansey's manner had changed. "Was it or was it not you who called 999 and said there was a bomb in the cloakroom of the Master's Lodgings here? Yes or no?"

"Yes — sir."

"How did you know?"

"Mr White — he's a Fellow of the College here — he came into the lodge and told me."

"So what did you do?"

"Mr White said to ring the police, which I did, and I sent Fairchild — that's my junior who's in hospital now, poor chap — to get everyone out of the Lodgings. But the bomb went off while he was at the front door."

"You were still here?"

"No. I was on my way across the quad to help Fairchild."

"And this Mr White? What did he do?"

"I've no idea, sir." It was a lie; Dobson had seen Greg White leave the College, but he had no intention of saying so. As he had told Ailsa Mackay, he didn't understand Mr White's behaviour, but he agreed with her implied suggestion that it wasn't up to him to tell tales to the police.

"I see," said Tansey thoughtfully. "And there's nothing more you can tell us that might help with our inquiries?"

"I don't think so, sir."

"I see," said Tansey again. "Well, many thanks — for the moment, Dobson." He turned to Abbot. "Sergeant, I think it's time we went and had a talk with the Bursar. And in the meantime we'll ask Inspector Carey to see if he can track down this Mr White."

★ ★ ★

Directed by Carey, they found the Bursar in his office on the ground floor of one of the front quad staircases. After Tansey had expressed his consternation at the attack on St Xavier's, he asked Mr Lacque about that morning's meeting.

"These meetings are held every other Monday in term-time," the Bursar explained. "They start punctually at nine-thirty and usually last an hour and a half to two hours, depending on the agenda. They're chaired by the Master, of course, and attended by his Secretary, Miss Mackay, the department heads, myself and often, if there's a particular problem to be discussed, one of the other Fellows."

"The routine was well known?"

"Throughout the College. Oh yes."

"And this morning's meeting was seemingly no different from any other?"

"In composition, no, though we were rather light on the ground — fortunately, as it happened. Let me see. Who was there? The Master, Miss Mackay, Dr Ansley, Dr Dawson, Mr Mead and myself. Mr Chapman, who's an athletic type, was painting his house over the weekend and fell off a ladder, so he had made excuses. Mr Beale's wife phoned to say he was laid low with a temperature. You've got all that?" He addressed the query to Abbot.

"Yes, sir. Thank you, sir," Sergeant Abbot acknowledged by holding up his notebook. "I can check the spelling of the names with the list of members of St Xavier's."

"Good. And Miss Mackay will provide any further details you need, and tell you about Mr White. I'd prefer she did that herself. He was due to attend the meeting but he never arrived."

The Bursar looked at his watch. "Chief Inspector, with the Master and Dr Dawson, the Senior Tutor, both in hospital I've a hundred and one things to see to, as you can imagine. Could we possibly continue this later? I'm sure there are other people you wish to interview."

"Of course, Mr Lacque. Thank you for

giving me such a clear general picture of the situation, but just one more question. Can you think of anyone who might have committed this crime?"

"No, I can't, Chief Inspector. We're a very peaceful College. We've never had any sort of political or racial trouble here."

The Bursar was clearly eager to leave, and Tansey didn't press the point, though he had not himself been thinking in such broad terms. He rose to his feet with Abbot and left the office.

Outside in the quad they found Inspector Carey waiting to escort them to the rooms that the College had set aside for the use of the police. They were normally used by a Dr Cathcart, who was in hospital recovering from peritonitis, and they overlooked the front quad from the ground floor of a staircase near the Bursar's office. The set consisted of two rooms, opening off a small hall, as did a small bathroom. The rooms were usually furnished as a study and a bedroom. Now a couple of uniformed constables were moving in desks and equipment from a van parked outside in the quad. The original study — the larger of the two — would become the incident room, and the bedroom Tansey's office and the interview room. Tansey nodded his approval.

"Mr White doesn't appear to be in the College, sir," said Carey. "At any rate, he can't be found. He was last seen heading towards the porter's lodge a few minutes before the incident. But Dobson wouldn't commit himself. I went over the same ground that you did, but all he'd say was that Mr White *might* have left the College. Dobson wasn't exactly cooperative."

Tansey grinned. "I noticed that too."

"I tried to phone the Whites' house — they live in North Oxford — but the line's dead. The phone company's looking into it. Shall I put out a call for this Mr White?"

"No-o. It's a bit soon. But you might send an officer out to the Whites to make sure everything's all right there. If White himself is at home bring him back here."

"Will do, sir. Here's WPC Robertson for you, sir." Carey held the door open for her.

"People are trickling back into College, sir, now that it's been searched," she said. "I've got the list of members — that was simple. I've also got a preliminary list of possible witnesses. It's long, sir, and still may not be complete, but I've done my best to sort out the ones you might like to see first. There's one young student, Peregrine Courcey, who claims to have witnessed 'the whole show' as he called it from the window of his rooms."

"Really? Sounds too good to be true."

"It probably is, sir," Abbot remarked cynically.

"Nevertheless, we'll have him in."

★ ★ ★

Peregrine Courcey proved to be an elegant character, who was not in the least abashed at being interviewed by two detective officers. He said good morning cheerfully, sat and crossed his long legs, carefully adjusting the creases in the trousers of the checked suit he was wearing. He also had an embroidered waistcoat and his hair was unfashionably shoulder-length. All in all, he looked more like a dilettante (in the true sense of the word, thought Tansey, who was keen on the correct usage of English) than an undergraduate.

"I saw it all," said Courcey, "or almost all. I had a wonderful view, a front seat in the dress circle, you might say." He gave his graphic description, and concluded, "I must admit those three chaps impressed me — dashing into the place to rescue people like that. There could easily have been another bomb."

Tansey glanced questioningly at his Sergeant, who referred to his notes. "Mr Hugh and Mr Richard Fremont, and Mr Anthony Pulent."

"That's right," Courcey continued. "Actually, they were jolly lucky. They were standing right by the wall that collapsed, when Greg White came out of the Lodgings. He spoke to them for a few moments. From his gestures it almost looked at if he was ordering them away — but they'll tell you about that, of course. If they'd not moved, they'd have been buried like the porter chap."

"Where did they go?"

"They just started to stroll across the quad, and then the bomb went off."

"And Mr White went with them, did he?"

"Oh no. He went over to the lodge."

"Was he carrying anything?"

The question puzzled Courcey. "What sort of anything?"

"Forget it. Would you say this was a quiet, peaceful college, Mr Courcey?"

The question was greeted with a hoot of laughter. "After this morning? You must be joking, Chief Inspector."

Tansey had not been joking. "Let me put it another way," he said. "You're in your fourth year here?"

"Yes. I'm reading Greats."

"Then you should know the place well. Would you say there was any element in St Xavier's College which felt strongly about politics or race or religion, for example?"

Courcey stared at Tansey. "You're thinking this was a terrorist bomb?" he asked. Then he added, "I doubt it, myself."

Sergeant Abbot was entertained to see that the Chief Inspector had been taken aback. Mr Peregrine Courcey might appear to be an elegant fop, but he wasn't lacking in imagination. Head on one side, he appeared to be considering the matter further. Tansey remained silent.

"Terrorism?" repeated Courcey at last. "No, Chief Inspector. We do have a certain number of chaps who aren't white Anglo-Saxon Protestants, and I myself wouldn't vote Conservative. But, praise be, there's never been any violence here till today, and if this was meant to be some kind of demonstration I can't imagine why an outsider should pick on us. To be honest, though we've been criticized for being fairly snobbish in our choice of undergraduates, in reality we're a pretty dim place — especially since people like Amanda Hulton and Hugh Fremont and that set went down."

"So who were Amanda Hulton and that set?"

Courcey considered the Chief Inspector for a moment. Then he said, "Well, I suppose *you* might have called us bright young things, Chief Inspector. I was one of them myself, though I wasn't their year. But I was at school with Hugh."

"I see," said Tansey. "So all you've said would suggest the bomb was a personal attack on the Master and those who attend these regular meetings."

"The hierarchy of St Xavier's? I suppose it would, Chief Inspector, but I couldn't begin to guess who'd do such a thing, or why."

"Well, thank you very much, Mr Courcey."

"My pleasure, Chief Inspector."

Tansey was thoughtful as Peregrine Courcey left. He had been impressed by the young man, whose instinct had helped to support his own growing belief that St Xavier's College had not been the victim of an act of terrorism, but of something more personal. For this reason his interest in Gregory White was increasing. There was still no news of White.

Courcey was followed by Hugh and Richard Fremont and Tony Pulent. As soon as they were seated, Tansey congratulated them on their efforts at rescuing the occupants of the Master's Lodgings. Then he asked, "Did Mr White say anything to you about a bomb when he came out of the Lodgings just before the explosion?"

There was a brief silence, then: "A bomb? Certainly not!" This from Hugh Fremont. "How could he know?"

"As I understand it, Mr White went straight from talking to you to the porter's lodge, where he told Dobson to call the police and warn everyone in the Lodgings." Tansey let them absorb this information which he suspected they were already aware of. "Are you sure he didn't warn you? Did he seem upset at all?"

"No." Hugh was casual. "I introduced my brother, whom he'd not met before, and we had a brief conversation. Incidentally, who says he told Dobson there was a bomb in the Lodgings?"

Tansey didn't answer. Instead he asked a question of his own. "Did you notice if he was carrying anything — a briefcase, say?"

"No," said Hugh Fremont.

"Yes," said his brother.

Tansey addressed Richard, whom he had recognized as the most vulnerable of the trio. "Do you mean Mr White

110

was carrying a briefcase?"

"I mean, I did notice, and he wasn't. I shook hands with him and I'd have seen it," Richard mumbled.

"What about you, Mr Pulent?"

Tony shrugged. "I didn't notice, but I can tell you one thing, Chief Inspector. If you're accusing Greg White of being responsible for that explosion, you're making a big mistake. I live next door to him and his family. I've known him all my life. And there's not a better man anywhere."

"I'd second that," said Hugh.

"I'm not accusing Mr White — or anyone else," Tansey said mildly. "It's much too early for anything like that. I'm just trying to build up a general picture of the quad and the incident."

This was not untrue, but clearly they didn't believe him. They answered the rest of his questions guardedly, almost sullenly, and he learnt nothing more of value from them. After they had left he turned to Abbot. "What do you think, Sergeant?"

"This Mr White seems an odd bloke."

"Quite," said Tansey shortly. "Let's

try the secretary. What's her name?" He looked at the list in front of him. "Ah, Ailsa Mackay, of course."

★ ★ ★

Ailsa Mackay proved a great help. Her files were in her office in the Master's Lodgings, but she had a good memory and without difficulty produced confirmatory information about those who had been present at the Monday meeting, and those who should have been there but for one reason or another had not attended. It was only when Tansey asked her to describe the events of the morning and mentioned Mr White that he sensed she had become wary.

"You say Mr White was the last to arrive. You met him in the hall. Was he carrying a bag?"

"His briefcase."

"Did you actually see him go into the cloakroom?"

"Yes. I watched him because . . . He'd said his inside was upset and he looked ill."

"You didn't see him leave the cloakroom?"

"No. I went into the Master's study. I expected Mr White to arrive, but he didn't. I imagine he didn't feel well enough. The meeting started and then there was this explosion."

Tansey, who felt rather sorry for the woman — her poor swollen face would have roused anyone's pity — thanked her. As she turned to go she glanced out of the window which gave a good view of the quad and the porter's lodge.

"Here's Mr White now — just coming into College," she said suddenly, unable to hide her relief.

8

GREG WHITE reached Broad Street with relief. He got in his car and automatically started for home, driving in a trance. It was not until he was turning off the Banbury Road that his mind cleared and it occurred to him that he was perhaps behaving foolishly. As far as he could recall there had been no sign that the white van had followed him home — in his dazed state he had forgotten to check whether or not it had gone from the place where he had last seen it outside Balliol — but the gunman whom he had left at his house might well still be there, ready to add his corpse to those of Jean and Rosemary. He had trusted the man because there had been no choice, but he need not walk into a trap now. He could go to a neighbour's — the Pulents, obviously — and call the police. But explanations would be complex and lengthy. Could his family wait? No. He must act himself, in case . . .

Nevertheless, he parked his car a little way along the road, and walked to the house. It looked quiet and peaceful, normal in every respect. If anyone had noticed that the curtains upstairs and downstairs were not yet drawn the fact probably wouldn't have been given a second thought. He went up the drive and cautiously circled the house. At the end of the sitting-room window most distant from the front door, a slight gap had been left in the curtains and he peered in.

"Oh no!" he said under his breath. "Please God, no!"

Rosemary was lying on the carpet. She was motionless and it was impossible for Greg to tell if she was breathing, but he could see that the manacles were still on her ankles.

Without further hesitation he ran to the front door and thrust his key into the lock, flung open the door — and stopped dead. Jean was lying on the floor of the hall in much the same position as her daughter.

But, hearing him, she had raised her head. "Greg!" she cried. "Thank God you're back! We thought you'd been — We thought you'd never come."

He knelt beside her. "Darling, are you all right?" It was a stupid question, but —

"Yes. Yes." Jean was impatient. "The man's gone. He went ages ago and he kept his promise; he didn't hurt either of us." Her voice rose to a shout. "Darling, it's Daddy. He'll get the keys."

"What keys?"

"The keys to these damned handcuffs, of course. The man said he'd leave them in the sitting-room. We waited and waited, but when no one came we decided to try to reach them ourselves." Jean was impatient. "But it's almost impossible to walk with one's ankles and hands chained like this. Rosemary was better at it than I was, which is why she's in there now."

"Hold on a moment."

Greg hurried into the sitting-room. "Oh, darling!" He gave Rosemary a brief hug. "The keys?"

"They're on the mantelpiece. I can see them, but I can't get to them."

Greg found the keys and, after

116

some fumbling, unlocked Rosemary's manacles. She rubbed her wrists and legs, and he lifted her up and sat her in an armchair.

"Be with you in a moment," he called to the hall.

"Dad!" Rosemary stopped him from leaving her. "The bomb? Did it explode? Was anyone hurt?"

"Later." Greg didn't wait. He had no wish to discuss the situation, not yet. "I must get your mother. We'll talk in a few minutes. Then I'll have to go."

"Go? Where?"

Greg didn't answer. He returned to the hall and freed Jean. He didn't know if it was because of his relief at finding them both safe and unharmed, but he suddenly felt exhausted. As he supported Jean into the sitting-room he noticed that the telephone socket had been ripped from the wall. It meant that he couldn't phone Lorna Pulent or anyone else for support, couldn't ask anyone to come and stay with Jean and Rosemary. On the other hand, he couldn't leave them alone. Nevertheless, it was vital that he returned to the College as quickly as possible. His first reaction to what had or had not been the results of the explosion had now been overcome by an urgent need to know the worst.

"I'm going to pop next door and fetch Lorna," he said. "She'll come and stay with you, keep you company. Would you like her to phone the doctor?"

"Greg, we don't want a doctor. And we don't want Lorna. First, make us some coffee and tell us what happened at St Xavier's. Then we'll get washed and dressed. We're quite all right now it's over, shaken naturally, but — "

"I can't leave you alone."

"We won't be alone. You'll be here — or are you going somewhere?"

"I must get back to the College."

"For God's sake, Greg, *why*? If people have been killed there's nothing you can do about it."

"Maybe I can help in some way, and in any case I have to talk to the police, tell them what I did. They'll want to talk to both of you too, I'm sure."

"But not immediately."

"The sooner the better. Those men

were dangerous. They've got to be caught."

"Of course, but — Greg, this has been a pretty harrowing experience for all of us. Surely we're entitled to a brief respite, just to be together for a few minutes as a family and feel safe again. It's not much to ask."

"Jean, there's something you should know, you and Rosemary. I didn't do exactly what they wanted. In the end, I couldn't." Greg thought for a moment of Ailsa Mackay. "If I'd left the briefcase in the study, I think everyone there would have been killed."

"So what *did* you do?" Jean's voice had become cold and distant.

"I put the briefcase in the downstairs loo at the Lodgings. I hoped it might save . . . And then as I left the College I warned Dobson, told him to call the police and get everyone out of the Lodgings before the bomb went off."

"Oh, Dad, that was clever of you — and brave." Rosemary, who had been listening intently, was admiring.

"It was neither clever nor brave! Don't be stupid, Rosemary! What your father did has put us all at risk again. Once those men discover he's deceived them, God knows what they'll do."

"I'm sorry, but I don't think it's as bad as that. They may not even find out. I was careful to make sure that there were no signs of an emergency before I'd left. That's one of the reasons I must get back to College, discover who — who was hurt, and what damage was done. A lot may depend on that. Then, as I say, I have to talk to the police — the senior officer — whoever's in charge there. Darling, try to understand."

"I understand all right." Jean rose to her feet. "But don't expect me to agree with you, Greg. Clearly we've got different priorities. So don't worry about us. I'll get the coffee and I'll cope here. You go back to your beloved College."

She stalked out of the sitting-room without a glance at him, and Greg sighed heavily. Jean didn't understand, he thought, but he couldn't blame her. He was not altogether sure that he understood himself. Perhaps he'd been wrong. "Perhaps I was a fool," he said aloud.

"No, Dad! No! You were right." Rosemary had no doubts.

She came to him and hugged him, and Greg thought that if anything happened to her — or to Jean — because of what he'd done, or not done, he would never forgive himself.

★ ★ ★

In fact, Greg did not leave home immediately, but forced himself to stay to drink coffee with Jean and Rosemary. He told himself that Jean was considerably more upset than she appeared to be on the surface, and that he owed it to her to give her love and support. But if his intentions were good, the results were the reverse. Jean remained bitter, and frightened at what might happen to them because of what she considered to have been Greg's uncompromising attitude. She refused to forgive him for not putting her and Rosemary first, before the welfare of his colleagues.

They bickered with ever-increasing intensity until Rosemary simply left them and went upstairs to dress. She still hadn't told them that she had seen Tom's face. Somehow there had never been a suitable moment before, and she realized that now it would be yet another bone of contention between her parents. Her father would feel she should tell the police; her mother, after the warning they had been given about not describing the gunmen, would want her to forget what she had seen. She heard the front door slam as she got under the shower, and she knew that her father had gone again.

He had not parted from Jean happily. Her last remark — indeed, it was a statement — still rang in his ears as he went towards his car. "Don't expect anyone except Rosemary to think you a hero, Greg. You've achieved exactly *nothing*! You've put your family in great danger again, and the chances are you'll be charged with blowing up the College and causing bodily harm — or worse — to your beloved colleagues, whom you care about more than your family. So let them visit you in prison, because I shan't."

Then Jean had picked up the coffee mugs and gone into the kitchen. He could hear her angrily stacking china and cutlery in the dishwasher, uncaring whether any piece became chipped or broken. He no longer cared, either. Without calling goodbye he went, slamming the front door behind him. As he got behind the wheel of his car he was shaking.

Until Jean's last virulent attack on him, it had not occurred to him to consider what the consequences of his actions might be for himself. His primary concern had been for Jean and Rosemary and the need to protect them; then he had done his best to save Ailsa and whomsoever might be in the study when the explosion took place. The fact that, according to Jean, he had failed in the first of these efforts made it even more important that he should find out what success he had achieved in the second.

So once again he set off for St Xavier's. Once again he was lucky and parked in Broad Street without any trouble, but he found his way barred half way down the Turl. The street was still cordoned off and traffic redirected along Ship Street, though members and staff had been allowed back into the adjoining colleges.

Obviously representatives of the media were there in force, though they too were compelled to remain outside the barricade.

It took Greg several minutes to persuade a police constable to allow him to go as far as St Xavier's lodge, and as he was allowed through, his passage was followed by the clicking of cameras.

In the lodge he was greeted by Dobson. "Mr White, am I glad to see you! Everyone's been looking for you, sir, asking where you'd got to." Dobson carefully didn't say, 'gone to'. He went on. "There's a Chief Inspector, name of Tansey, wants to speak to you. The Bursar set him and his sergeant up in Dr Cathcart's rooms."

"If you'd come along with me, please, sir." The police officer who was sharing the lodge with Dobson spoke politely but with authority. He had been warned that White might appear; the officer who had left for the Whites' house had phoned Inspector Carey to report that, according to Mrs White, her husband was on his way to the College.

"One moment!" Greg was adamant.

"Dobson — Dobson — was anyone badly hurt — or killed?"

"Not too badly, sir. Four of them have been hospitalized, but I gather they'll all survive."

"Thank God for that."

Greg felt weak. This was better news than he had dared to hope for; any damage to the Lodgings — and, looking across the quad, he could see from here that it was extensive — was insignificant beside the loss of life there might have been. The police officer was showing impatience, but Greg ignored him.

"Who?"

"The Master and Lady Pinel, sir, and the Senior Tutor and Fairchild. It's the young lad's situation that's the most worrying. He lives with his mother who's a bit of an invalid and — "

"Mr White, sir!" the police officer was becoming annoyed.

"I'm right with you. Don't worry, Dobson, I'll cope with the Fairchilds."

Greg followed the police officer across the quad. His thoughts were chaotic. He knew he should be concentrating on his coming meeting with this Chief Inspector

Tansey; he hoped the man would prove intelligent and understanding, and not be some blockhead eager for promotion. But his spirits had soared. No one had been killed. No one had been permanently maimed or Dobson would have said so. Almost euphoric in his relief, he bumped into Ailsa Mackay as she came out of the staircase he was entering.

"Greg! Are you all right?"

"Yes. I'm fine, but you — you — your poor face. My dear, I am sorry."

"It's not your fault. I'm sure of that, Greg."

Ailsa squeezed his arm, and gave him what she hoped was an encouraging smile though, distorted by her bruises, it was more like a grimace. But Greg knew what she was trying to convey, and he was grateful.

"Ailsa, I may be some time with the police. Could you arrange to let Fairchild's mother know what's happened, and give her whatever help's needed?"

"The police have already informed her and Hugh Fremont is driving Margaret Sandown out to Iffley, where the Fairchilds live." Miss Sandown was

126

a junior don. "She's a sensible girl. She'll cope."

"Good. I hope to see them as soon as I can. Meantime, if there's any question of money — "

"Greg, don't worry about the Fairchilds." Ailsa wanted to add, "And don't blame yourself, whatever's happened," but with the police officer standing near it didn't seem a politic comment.

★ ★ ★

"Chief Inspector, I'm the man responsible for planting that bomb in the lavatory of the Master's Lodgings."

Tansey hesitated for a moment, wondering about the applicability of the Judge's Rules in this unique and bizarre situation — a situation he had never before faced. Then he said, "May I take that as a voluntary confession, Mr White?"

"Certainly. But the act itself was the reverse of voluntary."

"Ah," said Tansey. "So — "

While Greg told his story Tansey and Abbot listened and observed. They noted

127

what appeared to be anomalies in his account. They noted how his voice broke when he described his fear for his daughter when she had been prevented from escaping. They noted the warmth with which he spoke of Ailsa Mackay and Tony Pulent, and his seeming restraint when he mentioned his wife. They noted his self-disgust at what he described as his own inadequacies, and his relief that no one had been killed or permanently maimed.

" . . . and that's about all I can tell you," Greg concluded.

Tansey sat quite still for a moment, considering. Then he glanced at Abbot, said 'Excuse me', and went through the hall into the incident room, where he found Inspector Carey. Briefly he passed on the story — was it a 'story', he wondered fleetingly, or was it the exact truth? — that Greg had told, and immediately gave his instructions.

"Get some uniformed men out to that house at once. Whatever the rights or wrongs of the matter, the occupants may be in danger. A marked car outside, and some uniformed men. And make sure one or two are armed. Then get a scene of crime team into the house. One of them can pick up White's dabs here. I know he says these gunmen wore gloves all the time, but they must have gone for a pee at least once, and you don't often keep gloves on for that. Get the loos checked for unusual prints. Get the place searched. Get those damned handcuffs White talks about — there should be four or six sets. See if there's anything to support White's story. But make sure no one questions his wife or daughter. I'll do that myself later."

"Will do, sir," said Carey laconically as Tansey went back to his office.

Here Greg and Abbot were sitting in an almost companionable silence. Tansey knew that Abbot had done the best possible thing, and made sure that White was relaxed and at his ease; that was just how he liked his witnesses — or suspects.

"Now, sir," he said, sitting behind his desk, "you remarked that you'd told us all you could, but I doubt it. Witnesses always know more than they think they do. Perhaps we could go through what you've said again. Then we'll have your statement typed and get you to sign it."

"Will it take long? I'm worried about my wife and daughter."

"Quite a time, I'm afraid. But don't worry about your family; they'll be taken care of." Greg looked up in surprise, but Tansey didn't answer the implied question. Instead, he said, "Let's start at the beginning again."

In fact, the process took longer than either of them expected, because Tansey found it necessary to interrupt frequently, so that the interview became an interrogation. When Greg hoped he had satisfied one query, there were always one or two more, such as precisely what he had said to Tony Pulent and the Fremont brothers.

"Why did you tell them to go to your rooms, Mr White?"

"It was the first thing that came into my head. I had to get them away from that wall."

"You didn't mind about Miss Mackay or your colleagues in the Master's study?"

"Of course I minded! Haven't I made that clear? But if I'd tried to warn them

130

they'd have come streaming out of the Lodgings and this Tom might have seen what was happening from outside the porter's lodge. I had to make sure he saw me come out of the College without the briefcase *before* the bomb went off. At that point there was every chance he'd make a getaway himself. Don't you see, I couldn't risk Rosemary and Jean. I've risked them too much anyway, or so Jean thinks, by not obeying orders, as it were."

It was an admission that explained some of the anomalies in White's story, and Tansey was becoming increasingly sympathetic with the man and his dilemma. Nevertheless, he had a job to do. Whatever White's motivation, he had committed a crime which might have produced an horrendous result.

"Mr White, I must ask you what I'm asking everyone. Do you know anyone who might have had a grudge against the Master, Sir Philip Pinel, or against St Xavier's?"

Greg wiped his brow with the back of his hand. He was tired. He had been woken shockingly in the early hours and had been under great strain ever since. Somehow during the Chief Inspector's questioning his euphoric relief that no one had been seriously injured had waned. By now he was having difficulty in thinking clearly.

"Not off-hand, Chief Inspector," he replied at last. "The Michaelmas Term has just started and the last university year was quiet and uneventful as far as I recall." Greg hesitated. "We did have a case of petty pilfering shortly before Christmas last year. It turned out to be one of the scouts and he was sacked, but — "

"His name?"

Greg shook his head. "I can't remember. He hadn't been with the College very long. Ailsa — Miss Mackay — would know. But isn't it a bit far-fetched to imagine — "

"We have to consider every possibility, Mr White. Is there anyone else you can think of?"

"No!" Greg regretted having mentioned the scout; clearly Ailsa had forgotten the incident, or not thought it worth mentioning.

"All right, Mr White. I'll pass you to Inspector Carey now. He'll arrange for your statement to be typed and get your fingerprints taken — for purposes of elimination when we go through your house. By that time Sergeant Abbot and I should be ready to call on your wife and daughter. You can come with us, and an officer will bring your car. Don't be surprised to find uniformed men on duty outside the house — you can guess why; in fact, you've already shown that you're aware of the possibilities. And there will be some officers examining the house, too, but they won't worry you. I'll be there myself to talk to your wife and daughter."

"Of course, Chief Inspector." Greg's smile was wry, as he wondered how Jean would accept the idea of house arrest.

9

TANSEY had declared a half-hour break from the interviewing, and on the Bursar's orders one of the scouts had brought soup, sandwiches and tankards of beer from the buttery to the set of rooms formerly occupied by Dr Cathcart. The Chief Inspector and his sergeant ate in silence. Abbot was thinking about his wife and his first child, soon to be born; Tansey was considering what Greg White had said, and its implications. It was this difference between them, as Bill Abbot had once humorously remarked, that had made Dick Tansey a Chief Inspector, while he himself remained a sergeant.

After the meal, at Inspector Carey's request, Tansey went out to make a brief statement to the media. A television crew had been allowed into the quad, and was busy filming the ruined frontage of the Master's Lodgings. Press and radio reporters — both locals and stringers from the national press — were questioning anyone who would talk to them, under the watchful eyes of a couple of uniformed officers. But as soon as Tansey appeared, they surged towards him, shouting their queries.

"How big was the bomb?" — "Who was it intended for?" — "Why St Xavier's?" — "Was it the IRA?" — "The Red Brigade?" — "What about casualties?" — "Anyone killed?" — "Who was hurt?" — "Any ideas yet?"

Tansey held up a hand. "I always have ideas, but at this stage I prefer to keep them to myself. It's only a few hours after the incident, so I'd have to be a genius to answer all your questions. I hope that tomorrow I'll be able to give a full press conference. Meanwhile, I'll tell you two things. First, four people have been hospitalized — including the Master of St Xavier's College and his wife — but I understand that none of them is in any serious danger. Secondly, I'll hazard a guess: this was not the work of any terrorist or political organization, but of two or three individuals who had some personal reason for their action."

In the surprise which greeted his last comment Tansey was able to make his escape and return to his room. He knew that he would be quoted, and probably misquoted, and that if his guess — which after all was no more than a reasonable surmise — proved to be wrong, he would have to bear the brunt of the criticism that would inevitably follow.

★ ★ ★

Tansey found Dr Ansley and Mr Mead waiting for him. In appearance they made a somewhat comical duo. Desmond Ansley was a tall, almost gaunt-looking man in his fifties; Brian Mead, not yet forty, was short and podgy, with a round baby face. Although physically unharmed except for a few superficial cuts from the shattered study window, they had both suffered from shock and had done their best to recover from it by a large intake of wine during lunch. As a result, though they were not drunk, they were by no means totally sober.

Tansey listened patiently while, in a kind of double act, the two dons described their experiences before and immediately after the explosion. He complimented them on their behaviour in rescuing Dr Dawson and asked them some general questions. He had little hope of learning anything fresh from them, but in this he was proved wrong. They had had time to consider the situation and, being far from stupid, had come up with some interesting ideas.

"Terrorism in some form would appear to be the obvious answer," said Ansley, "but we decided to reject it. We couldn't imagine any terrorist group worth its salt planting a bomb in the Master's downstairs loo."

He paused while Tansey waited, and eventually continued, "Look, we know it's no joking matter, but — the downstairs loo, where it would do the least harm. The idea's almost laughable. And even if one or two of us had been killed, what on earth would have been achieved? As far as we know, none of those in the study has even been involved with politics or the armed forces or even the police."

"The alternative would seem to be

someone with a grudge against the College in general, or the Master as a symbol of the College," Mead intervened. "If it were against any particular senior member other than Sir Philip, it would have been much simpler to attack him — or her — at home, rather than in the Master's Lodgings. On the other hand, as the day and time were clearly chosen so that the explosion would coincide with the start of one of our regular meetings, it's arguable that the Master was not the sole target."

"Quite," said Tansey. "There's a good deal in what you say. In fact, my own thoughts have been running along similar lines." Ansley and Mead exchanged satisfied glances. Then Tansey, expecting a largely negative reply, added, "And have you any suggestion as to who might be the — the culprit or culprits?"

"Several," they replied in chorus.

Tansey hid his surprise. "Then perhaps you'd be good enough to elucidate."

"Certainly," said Ansley. "Between us we've gone back over our memories of the last university year and, as I said, we've come across several possibles.

Mind you, Chief Inspector, some are more 'possible' than others."

"That's understood," said Tansey a little impatiently.

"Well, we begin with Harry, who was a scout at the College. We can't remember his surname, but Miss Mackay will know. Just before last Christmas there was a spate of pilfering from undergraduates' rooms. It was finally traced to Harry, and he was kicked out."

"Prosecuted?"

"No. The Master decided that a prosecution would create bad publicity for the College. Harry was a poor wretch, and there were extenuating circumstances."

"There always are," said Mead. "Extenuating circumstances, I mean. Personally, I think we made a mistake. We heard afterwards that Harry was swearing in his local that he was innocent, and he'd make the Master regret sacking him."

"He might have been drunk," Tansey commented, "but we'll look into him. Who else?"

Ansley and Mead again exchanged glances — this time almost mischievous glances — and Tansey began to think that, however clever the two dons might be, they were taking an almost childish delight in analysing the situation and were welcoming this opportunity to outline the latest College scandals. Mead belched gently and gave a self-satisfied smirk, somehow implying that he was responsible for the next suggestion though he would allow Ansley, as his senior, to offer it.

"Then, in the Hilary Term we had a spot of bother with drugs. Nothing unusual in that these days, of course, but not to be countenanced, nevertheless." Ansley spoke ruminatively. "Oddly enough, or so it seemed to me at the time, those involved were a dull bunch. I don't mean academically. I mean they were hard-working, serious types — the kind who finish up with good Second Class degrees if they're lucky. None of your gilded youth."

"We did have a small coterie of those," Mead remarked. "You know, the sort who never appear to do any work, but manage to finish up with good Firsts all the same. Bright in every way. But they nearly all went down the summer of last year. Most of them — like Hugh Fremont and the Hulton girl — got plum jobs, largely provided by rich and influential parents or relations." Mead sounded vaguely envious.

"Anyhow, they're irrelevant," Ansley interrupted. "And frankly I can't see any of our druggies planting a bomb in the Lodgings. Certainly not Davies."

"Who's Davies? And why not him?" Tansey asked quickly.

"Ah! Apparently Davies was the supplier. He and his girlfriend were both sent down. We don't know what happened to her, but Davies continued in his bad ways and your people caught up with him. He's now doing seven years. The others who were involved were rusticated for the rest of the term, but were allowed to return to take their Schools — their final examinations — so they really have no cause for complaint. In my opinion the College was pretty lenient — too lenient — with them."

"You didn't inform the police?" asked Tansey curtly.

"No, we didn't," Ansley admitted.

"Perhaps if you'd been less lenient and done so, Davies's career might have been cut off sooner," said Tansey. "Or was this another example of St Xavier's avoiding adverse publicity?"

Sergeant Abbot coughed loudly. He knew that the Chief Inspector held strong views about drug pushers, and he himself shared his superior's views, but it was not advisable to antagonize witnesses of this kind. Both Dr Ansley and Mr Mead had already become more reserved.

"No one likes bad publicity, Chief Inspector — not even the police force."

"Granted, Dr Ansley. However — have you thought of anyone else who might have a chip on his or her shoulder? People might have been employed to manufacture and place the bomb, we must remember."

Mr Mead opened his mouth and shut it quickly as Dr Ansley shook his head. Tansey cursed himself. He hadn't needed Abbot's warning cough to know that he had made a mistake.

"Would you say that Sir Philip Pinel was a popular Master?" Tansey tried a different tack. "I gather it's only five years since his election. Was it welcomed in the Senior Common Room?"

"The Senior Common Room elected him," said Ansley. "But opinions varied, all the same. The Master is an administrator — as indeed he needs to be — but there were some who considered that his academic qualifications were rather inadequate. Nevertheless, the College has flourished under his guidance."

"Do you know of anyone who was passed over in Sir Philip's favour, as it were — anyone who might be bitter about that kind of thing?"

Ansley shrugged. "People always have aspirations, but — no." Suddenly he smiled, showing large uneven teeth. "If you're thinking of Mr White, the answer's still in the negative. I'd say that Greg White's wife is considerably more ambitious than he is."

"Why should I be thinking of Mr White in particular?"

"It was he who went to the cloakroom in the Lodgings and then warned Dobson about the bomb, though much too late to be any use, wasn't it? Why didn't he warn us himself? It would have been vastly quicker."

So the grapevine was already at work, Tansey thought, and gossip was spreading. He felt sorry for Greg White; the man was going to have to take a lot of shit in the next few days and weeks. "So have you any reason to believe that Mr White had a grudge against the Master?"

"None!" Ansley admitted at once.

"None!" Mead echoed firmly.

Tansey got to his feet. "Well, thank you very much for your help, gentlemen. I may have to talk to you again, but for the moment, that'll do. Of course, if you think of anything else, however trivial, you can always get in touch with me through Inspector Carey, or the incident room we've set up next door."

The two dons rose. Standing side by side they made a ludicrous pair, but Tansey knew they were not to be underrated. They were intelligent men, and men with principles. As they reached the door he saw rather than heard Brian Mead murmur something

144

to his colleague, and Ansley stopped, turned and came back into the room to confront Tansey.

"Mr Mead has just reminded me, Chief Inspector," he said smoothly. "Last term there was some trouble over one of our women dons. I don't know the ins and outs of the matter, so I won't attempt to tell you about it. It may not be relevant — most probably it isn't — but if you're interested Miss Mackay would know the details."

* * *

"The answer to all our questions would seem to be Miss Mackay," Tansey said as soon as Ansley and Mead had left. "Unfortunately I'm not sure that at present she's being totally candid with us. A little ingenuous, would you say, Abbot?"

Detective-Sergeant Abbot, who was used to these sudden ruminative questions on the part of the Chief Inspector, merely nodded, and Tansey went on, "Still, I'd be interested to see her reactions to the names of the potential villains that have been suggested. We'd better have her in again."

"Now, sir? Time's getting on."

"I'm afraid so. It's going to be a long day. But we can't keep White and his family waiting indefinitely. We'll be as quick as we can."

"I'll get someone to fetch Miss Mackay, sir."

Stifling his reluctance, Abbot went across the small hall to the incident room, in what had been Dr Cathcart's sitting-room. How well these dons did themselves, he thought — good pay, long vacations, no shift work, freedom to set their own hours within reason and bags of prestige — very different from being a cop, even a Chief Inspector. And their wives were luckier, too.

Greg White looked up hopefully as the sergeant came into the incident room, where he was waiting, but when he heard Abbot ask for Miss Mackay, he returned to the magazine he was pretending to read. He had protested several times that he must return to his wife and daughter; each time he had been met with polite sympathy, but the comment that the

Chief Inspector was anxious that they should go back to North Oxford together. By now his statement had been typed, read and signed, but that had made no difference. Inspector Carey had assured him that his house and his family were under police protection and he need not worry about them. But how could he not worry? The minutes dragged.

"Miss Mackay has gone home to change her soiled clothes and have a bit of a rest," Inspector Carey was telling Abbot. "She'll be back later."

"Can I help?" The Bursar, who had entered the room and heard the exchange, addressed the Sergeant. "I can spare some time now."

"Chief Inspector Tansey has some queries that he hoped Miss Mackay could assist us with, sir, but perhaps you — "

"I'll do my best."

Peter Lacque followed the Sergeant out of the interview room, and Abbot explained the situation to Tansey. The Chief Inspector was more than happy. He had found Ailsa Mackay with her swollen face and wary, slightly uncooperative attitude less easy to deal with than the Bursar.

"Mr Lacque," he began, "what's your opinion of Mr White?"

The Bursar was taken aback. "Were you intending to ask Ailsa Mackay that?"

"I'm asking you — and it's a serious question."

"Worthy of a considered reply?" The Bursar took the minor snub in good part. "Right. Let me marshal my thoughts." The Bursar was a small man, with heavy tortoiseshell-rimmed spectacles too large for his face. He paused for only a moment. "Greg White has been a Fellow of this College for about twenty years. I've known him for ten. He's a conscientious tutor and a good teacher. He's popular with his pupils, but some of the Senior Common Room despise him because he publishes very little — if any — original work of his own. I'd say that during his time here he's served St Xavier's extremely well."

"I see. And as a person? Would you call him a friend, for instance?"

"I'd be proud to do so, Chief Inspector. I know there's a wild rumour going around the College that he dashed out of the Lodgings without warning those of us in the Master's study. The gossip has various versions. Frankly, I don't believe any of them. Greg wouldn't save himself at someone else's expense. He's not that kind of man. He'd be much more likely to throw himself on a live hand grenade so as to save others. I can only believe that, if there's any truth in the gossip at all, Greg White was acting under some greater compulsion."

For a minute Tansey was silent. He was impressed by what the Bursar had said — and by his concluding sentence. It confirmed his own opinion, but, coming from an individual who had known White for many years, was a most useful endorsement. He decided to retail to Lacque the version of events that White had provided.

"Good God! It's unbelievable! So I was getting close to the truth," Lacque said as Tansey finished. "And, if that's what Greg White maintains, I believe him. But who the hell are these men? And why should they — ?"

These were obviously rhetorical questions, but Tansey chose to answer them. "Villains with a grudge against St Xavier's would satisfy both your points, wouldn't they, Mr Lacque? I've been offered various suggestions and I'd like to know what you think of them."

The Bursar listened carefully as Tansey outlined what he had been told. "All right," he said, "I'll give you my comments. The scout — his name was Harry Batsford — was a youth with an unfortunate background and I'm glad he wasn't prosecuted. I believe he's been going straight since he left here. He's working in a garage in Cowley, I gather. There's no way I can imagine him undertaking a crime like this.

"The drug business was a different matter. I think we — those of us in the College with responsibility, and among those I include myself — behaved atrociously. We should have disregarded the possibility of publicity and called in the police, but the Master wouldn't have it. Davies was a bad lot. So was his girlfriend, one Betty Fergus. But Davies is in prison now. I don't know what's happened to Fergus."

"We'll have to look into them — and Batsford."

"Of course."

Tansey waited, but the Bursar volunteered no more, and the Chief Inspector had to prompt him. "Any other hidden scandals, Mr Lacque?"

The Bursar shook his head, and then stared at Tansey in some surprise. "You're not thinking of poor Emma Watson, are you?" he asked. "If you are, you have been raking through our dirty linen, Chief Inspector."

"Just tell me about Emma Watson."

"She was a history don, early thirties, very attractive — too attractive for her own good, perhaps. In many ways we're a small-minded, closed community." Lacque paused, and then went on. "Anyway, Emma became pregnant. There were several rumours as to the father." He hesitated again. "In the end, she — she lost the baby, and was quite ill. She didn't come back to the College. She's teaching in a school in Abingdon."

"I see," said Tansey, who didn't really see the relevance of the Watson story.

In any case time was pressing and he must get away to the Whites' home. Deliberately he looked at his watch. "Time we were off, Mr Lacque. We'll be back tomorrow, no doubt. Meanwhile, thanks for your help. I shall probably need it again. Contact Inspector Carey if you're worried about anything in the meantime."

The Bursar nodded. "Anything I can do, Chief Inspector — I want this business cleared up as much as you do."

But it was not going to be simple, Tansey thought. The Chief Constable had been right. The case, even on the first day, showed every sign of becoming curious and complex.

10

"IN the back, if you will, Mr White." Greg climbed into the rear of the unmarked police car, thankful that the waiting was over and at last he was on his way home. Tansey, glad of a respite, however brief, from the chore of interviewing, got in beside him. Abbot drove, with beside him a police constable who was to drive Greg's car to his house. Greg had already handed over his keys.

"That's it. That old red Ford Fiesta," Greg said as they reached Broad Street.

Abbot, regardless of the traffic rules, drew up directly in front of the Ford. The police constable got out, walked around the car, glanced underneath and was about to open the door when Greg made an inarticulate sound, and pointed.

"You bloody people have made me get a parking ticket!" he cried.

Tansey drew a deep breath. "Mr White, we're not as used to dealing with explosives as you appear to be. For a split second I thought you'd spotted some sort of device — a booby trap, perhaps. It was a nasty moment."

"I'm sorry. But it's damned annoying."

"Not to worry. I'll fix your parking ticket if I have to pay it myself."

"Good! I'll keep you to that, Chief Inspector."

Tansey grinned. He was beginning to like Greg White and, as he learnt more about him, he was also beginning to trust him — and his account of recent events. The man was clearly under a great strain, and it was difficult to believe that, in the circumstances, if he were acting he could be so convincing. Nevertheless, Tansey reminded himself that he must keep an open mind; if they found — as he personally hoped they would — corroborative evidence of White's story at his house, it would be a different matter. He signalled to Abbot, who drove off, leaving the Fiesta to follow, and it was not until they neared their destination that Tansey spoke again.

He said, "Mr White, as I mentioned earlier, I'm afraid you'll find that your home's rather full of police, and there'll be a couple of our cars outside. They're there partly to protect your family, just in case — "

"In case of what?"

"Oh, come on, Mr White, you know what I mean. In fact, you've hinted at the possibility yourself. In case these men take further action once they've realized that their bomb hasn't been entirely successful. Though as they must also realize that by this time you've told your tale to the police, I should think they'd have to be very stupid or very determined to do anything but lie low."

"Of course you're right, Chief Inspector. You were saying — "

"And partly to search for clues to help us with our investigation."

"I understand."

"Of course you'll want to greet your wife and daughter. After that I shall have to ask you to wait with Sergeant Abbot, while I hear what my men have to say. Then I'll talk to your family."

Greg nodded. He knew he had no choice, so there was no point in objecting to this procedure. But after the harrowing experiences of the morning he seemed to have done nothing but wait and, though he hated to admit it, he didn't altogether trust Jean to be fully cooperative with Tansey.

His misgivings increased when they arrived at the house. Jean gave him a cool cheek to kiss, and barely acknowledged the Chief Inspector and Abbot. He was glad to turn to Rosemary, who hugged him, then offered her hand to both police officers. Reluctantly he left them and showed Abbot to his study.

"Obviously I want to talk to you, Mrs White," Tansey said, "and to Miss White, but first I must speak to my colleagues."

"Is my husband under arrest?"

"Good heavens, no! Most certainly not."

"Just helping you with your inquiries?" Jean was sarcastic.

Tansey's smile was thin, but all he said was, "I shan't be long, Mrs White."

He found the inspector in charge of the scene of crime team in the kitchen, with the uniformed senior constable in charge of the protective squad. The scene of crime officer was a small, morose character, who was rarely happy whatever incriminating evidence his men managed to uncover.

"Any joy?" Tansey asked him.

"Not really, sir." He lowered his voice and pointed vaguely in the direction of the sitting-room. "That stupid — lady! The villains drank tea and ate toast. Maybe they kept their gloves on, but there could have been saliva, for example — and what does the lady do? As soon as she can she puts all the damned crockery into the dishwasher! There it is — it's just finished swishing away the evidence. We got here much too late to stop her."

"Too bad!" Tansey refused to commiserate further. "What about prints elsewhere?"

"There are plenty all over the place. Presumably the family. At first the — lady objected to having her dabs taken, but I persuaded her; the girl was amused and interested. But there'll be a lot of elimination to do — the cleaning woman, friends, relations, odd callers. There are some prints that seem to recur a good deal, so that's likely to be a frequent visitor. The girl's boyfriend, perhaps. Even if we can't place them all, there's no guarantee that the ones that we're left with belong to the villains," he added gloomily. "Incidentally, there are a lot of smudges that we guess have been left by gloved fingers. I think our chummies were very, very careful."

"So?" said Tansey.

"Well, it's obvious, sir. *If* you catch anyone, and *if* they've been careless — in a bathroom, for instance — the dabs here might help. Otherwise . . . "

Tansey noted the officer's pessimism, but he didn't comment. Clearly the bathrooms had been checked, and he knew better than to ask about the toilet and its flushing handle. However discouraging the man might be, no one had ever found cause to doubt his efficiency.

"Right," Tansey said. "Anything else? What about those cuffs that White talks of?"

"Oh, we've got those all right. They're cheap objects — almost the kind you might buy in a joke shop. Fair enough for the job they had to do, though given a little time any professional would manage to free himself. Hard to trace, too, sir; I should be very surprised if they provided any useful information."

"I'm sure you're right." Tansey suppressed a sigh.

"Before we go we'll show you how we think the men got in, and probably out, sir? OK?"

"Fine. I'd like to have a look around by myself first."

Tansey gave instructions to the constable about protective arrangements for the Whites, and then left the kitchen, seeking to acquaint himself with the layout of the house in order that he might better understand the sequence of events that morning. He walked around the dining-room and went upstairs. He found the Whites' bedroom, came out into the passage, and glanced into a room that was obviously Rosemary's. He spent a few minutes in the bathroom from which she had tried to escape, inspecting the broken door bolt and studying the view from the window. The girl, he thought, had guts and so, in his way, had her father — if his story was true; and indeed everything he had seen in the house up to now appeared to confirm it.

Slowly Tansey went down the stairs. As he reached the last step a young uniformed WPC came into the hall. She looked pleased.

"Sir, I'm one of the team looking after the Whites — they thought a woman officer should be here. But I think I've discovered how those men got in. Would you like to see? Or have you been told already, sir?"

"Lead on, Constable." Tansey, amused by her enthusiasm, was not prepared to frustrate her.

She led the way through the kitchen to a utility room which contained a washing machine and a tumble-drier, just leaving enough space for an ironing board to be erected. The room, though small, had a surprisingly large, low window.

"It's made like that so on a fine day you can lean out of the window and hang up your washing, which dries much fresher in the open air than in a machine," the girl explained earnestly.

Tansey, who was a married man and a recent father, refrained from saying that he had much the same arrangement in his own house. He stared at the latch which, like most of the others in the Whites' home, was far from secure. Then he caught his breath. The wretched girl had undone the window, flung it open and was leaning out.

"It's OK, sir." She gave him a wide smile to which he didn't respond. "The whole surroundings have been checked over, no prints, but a couple of black threads caught on a nail. Incidentally, the villains came in this way, but almost certainly went out by the side door. It locks itself, but there's a bolt inside and that was open. Mrs White assured us the door was properly locked up when they went to bed last night, but — "

"Right." Tansey just saved himself from appearing brusque. Somehow the girl, with her obvious determination to impress him with qualities which might lead her into the CID, made him feel old. He began to turn away, but he was not an ungenerous man, and he remarked, "Good work!" before he moved off.

"Thank you, sir."

Tansey went through the kitchen into the hall. The scene of crime team had now finished and were packing up their gear. He spoke to the officer in charge, saying that he'd been shown the utility room. The officer, as expected, was not hopeful that any really useful evidence had been unearthed, though he was prepared to admit that what had been found tended to support rather than dispute White's story.

And now for Mrs White, Tansey thought. Squaring his shoulders as if to gear himself to face a difficult encounter, he entered the sitting-room where Jean and Rosemary sat in an uncompanionable silence, pretending to read.

* * *

"I'm sorry to have kept you so long, Mrs White."

"That's all right, Chief Inspector. We're not going anywhere — unless you intend to take us to some police station."

"Why should I do that?"

"To charge us with being accessories to a crime, of course," Jean snapped.

"Accessories? Not victims, Mrs White?"

Jean didn't answer. She carefully put a

marker in the book and shut it. Tansey noticed that she was pale, and her hands were shaking slightly. Rosemary, on the other hand, seemed to be reasonably relaxed.

"Mrs White, I'd like you to tell me what happened from the time you heard a noise downstairs in the middle of last night."

"Surely my husband's told you all that already."

"Yes, naturally. But you may be able to fill in more detail — and I hope that Miss White will help too."

"I'll try," said Rosemary.

"Rosemary! Don't — don't start inventing things." Jean gave Tansey a weak smile and waved him to a chair. "The young are so fond of dramatizing," she said.

Tansey nodded an agreement that he didn't feel. Jean White, he decided, was frightened, probably more for her family and her home than for herself. He took it for granted that the villains had threatened dire consequences if the Whites provided any evidence against them.

163

"Well, I woke my husband — " Jean began.

Tansey listened attentively. Her account, which grew less hesitant and more fluent as it continued, differed from her husband's only in emphasis.

In conclusion, she let her feelings show. She reiterated, "As I said, Greg had no choice though he seemed to think he had, but really it was either doing what these men ordered, or letting Rosemary and me be killed — and probably raped first. Of course he didn't want to blow up the Master and the other people at that meeting, but — " she shrugged angrily. "Well, in the end he didn't, did he? His courage failed him. God knows what will happen to us all now!"

"Mrs White, until these men are caught, or we believe they've ceased to be a danger, you and your family will have police protection, I assure you."

Jean laughed. "Chief Inspector, I must speak candidly. In my opinion your assurance is worth precisely nothing. Police protection's a joke — and as for these men being caught, I suspect the likelihood of that is minute."

"I hope you've misjudged the situation, Mrs White," Tansey said soberly, and thought he understood why she was afraid; she had reached the conclusion that the villains might try to take vengeance for the minimal success of their plan, and indeed he had to admit it was a possibility. But it seemed grossly unfair of her to blame her husband. "However, to continue — "

"I don't agree with my mother!" Rosemary could contain herself no longer. "Dad was great, Chief Inspector! He did everything he could, everything right when those ghastly men were here. Actually, the oldie wasn't too bad, but that disgusting Tom!"

"Rosemary!"

Rosemary paid no attention to Jean. "As for Dad putting the bomb in the loo, that was a brilliant idea. A part of the Lodgings may have got destroyed, but it's only a modern building anyway and no one was seriously hurt. What else could he have done, Chief Inspector? What would you have done in Dad's place?"

"I don't know, Miss White." Tansey

hesitated, then replied honestly. "Tell me about this Tom. You struggled with him on the bathroom floor. Did his breath smell — of tobacco or liquor or chewing gum, say?"

Rosemary shook her head. "Not that I noticed."

"Did you notice anything particular about either of them — any mannerisms, for example? What about you, Mrs White?"

"No, nothing!" Jean spoke too quickly.

"You must have got some impression of them."

"They were dressed from head to toe in black. The older one — at least the one who seemed to be in charge — was short and square. Tom — if that was his real name — was taller and thinner. At the time they were horrible, terrifying! They threatened us. But they did make us tea and toast, and in the end they *kept their word*. They said they had nothing against us, and wouldn't hurt us if we followed their instructions — and they didn't. Of course when the older one left here he didn't know what Greg had done."

"They sound an unusual couple," said Tansey mildly. He was tempted to add that Mrs White sounded as if she were siding with the villains rather than the forces of law and order. Certainly she was not being helpful. And he had noted the emphasis she had put on the phrase 'they kept their word', clearly implying that her husband had not.

"It's interesting that they denied having anything against Mr White," he commented. "I don't think he mentioned that point. Mrs White, would you say these men were acting on their own behalf, or were being paid to do a job?"

"It was their own show!" Rosemary answered before Jean had time to give a shrug to express ignorance. "It was some personal matter to them, I'm sure."

"Why? What makes you so sure?"

"I — I don't know."

"Rosemary dear, really! You must not pretend you know things when you don't. I'm sorry, Chief Inspector."

Tansey waved aside Jean's apology on behalf of her daughter. He grinned at Rosemary. "A funny internal feeling, eh? I get them myself sometimes."

Rosemary returned his grin. "A strong feeling," she said, and gave her mother a challenging glance.

"OK." Tansey didn't want to exacerbate the festering disagreement between mother and daughter. "Now — " He stopped. Rosemary had made an inarticulate sound. "What is it?"

"Chief Inspector, when you said 'OK' just now, it reminded me. And I'm not making it up. You can ask Dad. Both Tom and the other man kept saying 'oke' instead of 'OK'. They repeated it several times. Of course, I've heard people say 'oke', but not all the time, and not recently."

"Do you recall that, Mrs White?"

"Yes," Jean said reluctantly. "But I doubt if it's important. Lots of people use out of date slang."

"It helps to build up a picture," Tansey said, and thought that it was turning out to be a damned funny picture. "Now, what about their voices?"

"Not particularly well educated, but of course they were distorted by their masks." Jean was giving away as little as possible.

"And is there anything else either of you can tell me?"

Tansey looked hopefully from Jean to Rosemary; as he had expected, the interview had been hard going. They both shook their heads, but Rosemary gave him a curious stare that he couldn't interpret. He wondered if she did have further information that she wasn't prepared to mention in front of her mother.

"Then we'll call it a day, Mrs White — Miss White. If anything else does occur to you, you know how to get in touch with me. Meanwhile, thank you both very much for your help. Incidentally, there'll be two officers — a constable and a WPC — inside your house overnight, and another in a police car in the street, so I trust you'll be quite safe. Not that I think you need expect any trouble, but it's a form of insurance."

Tansey stood up. Mindful of the lectures that he occasionally had to give to new recruits on the importance of maintaining good relations with the public, he suppressed his personal feelings and ignored Mrs White's studied silence. "I'll say goodbye then, for the present."

Neither of them answered, though Jean gave him what could only be called a nod of dismissal, and Rosemary produced a rather worried smile. He left the room thoughtfully, to encounter Greg White coming out of the downstairs cloakroom. "Ah," he said, "I wanted a word with you before I go. I think we'd better have a tap on your phone, which'll be repaired any minute now. It'll mean having another officer in the kitchen with an instrument and a recorder. You and your family can answer the phone as usual. My man will only intervene or record if the call's other than personal."

"Fair enough," replied Greg. "Have you told my wife?"

"No," said Tansey. "I thought I'd leave that to you." He gave Greg a sympathetic glance before he continued, "And what about tomorrow? I take it you'll want to go in to St Xavier's."

"Yes, naturally," said Greg, surprised.

Tansey sighed. "OK. I'll have a man with you all the time."

As he went out he was reflecting that

he was now convinced that Greg White's account of events had been truthful, and for that at least he was grateful. One obstacle on the way ahead had been cleared.

11

A T two o'clock the following morning, Dr Harold Dawson, the Senior Tutor of St Xavier's College, died as a result of a second — and this time massive — coronary. The staff at the hospital did everything they could to save his life, but to no avail. His wife and son had been hurriedly summoned, but arrived too late to see him alive. Mrs Dawson was unexpectedly bitter. Unrestrained in her grief, she loudly blamed the College for their slack security precautions which had enabled someone to plant a bomb in the Master's Lodgings, thereby causing her husband's first heart attack and subsequently his death. She threatened to sue, though on precisely what grounds was not clear. She became hysterical, declaring that 'dear Harold' had been murdered.

Eventually, escorted by her son and a nurse, the unhappy widow went sobbing along a corridor to the lifts. In spite of their efforts to calm her, she made a considerable amount of noise — enough to wake one of the patients in a small ward nearby.

That patient was Bert Fairchild, the junior porter at St Xavier's. He had remembered nothing of what had happened from the time he had dashed across the quad on Dobson's orders to warn everyone in the Lodgings that there was a bomb in the toilet, until he had found himself in hospital with a broken leg, multiple bruising, several cracked ribs and concussion, and had been told about the explosion. He was in a great deal of pain, but an injection had helped, together with some sedatives, and he had managed to get a little rest. But once he had been woken by the weeping Mrs Dawson, he had been far too uncomfortable to manage any more sleep.

Hoping to find comfort in a chat with a nurse, and perhaps a hot drink even if he were not allowed another injection or more pills, Fairchild rang the bell. It was several minutes before a nurse appeared; the hospital was having a busy night. But Fairchild didn't mind waiting.

He considered that he had been treated extremely well since his arrival at the hospital — almost like a hero — and once he had learnt that his own injuries were considerably more serious than those suffered by anyone else involved in the bomb incident, he had allowed himself to relax. After all, he reflected, if he had done wrong no great harm had come of it, and he was suffering more than others. It didn't occur to him that this was a very specious argument.

A nurse appeared eventually, promised him a glass of hot milk and went away again. Fairchild dozed, in spite of his discomfort. Hot milk reminded him of his old mum. He had been glad to see her yesterday afternoon. It had been good of Mr Fremont and Miss Sandown to bring her, very kind. Then there had been messages from Miss Mackay that he was not to worry — about his mother, his job or anything; the College was grateful for what he had tried to do, and she could assure him that it would show its gratitude.

Fairchild winced suddenly. He had shifted his position in the bed, and a pain shot though his chest. He swore vividly under his breath: these damned ribs; they were quite the most uncomfortable of his injuries. He was sorry that Ailsa Mackay had been hurt; she was a nice lady. As for Miss Sandown, he rather fancied her, but he knew he wouldn't stand a chance against someone like Hugh Fremont. Apart from anything else, Fremont already owned a sports car, and she wouldn't want to ride on the motorbike that he, Bert Fairchild, was trying to save for with so much effort. He was dreaming of the Yamaha TZR that was almost within his reach when the nurse returned.

"Here we are," she said cheerfully, but in a whisper so as not to wake the other patients on the ward. "But I don't know what you think you're doing, pretending you can't sleep after all the drugs you've been given."

"I *was* asleep until there was a lot of noise in the passage outside; it sounded like a woman crying her eyes out."

"Oh yes, poor Mrs Dawson."

"Dawson?" Fairchild nearly choked on his milk. "You don't mean Dr

Harold Dawson's wife? Why should she be crying? Has anything happened to him?"

The nurse was nearing the end of her shift, and because the floor was short of staff she was tired, and she momentarily forgot that her patient and Dr Dawson were victims of the same outrage. "I'm afraid Dr Dawson died a short while ago," she said quietly.

"Died? How did he die? He was — "

"He had what you would call a major heart attack."

"But it was the result of that explosion, wasn't it? Wasn't it?" Fairchild insisted. "If it hadn't been for the bomb he wouldn't have died." His voice had risen.

"Mr Fairchild, please!" The nurse gave no direct reply, but took the half-empty glass away from him. "Speak quietly and don't get so excited, or I'll have to send for a doctor."

Fairchild didn't answer. He had pulled the sheet up over his face. He didn't want the nurse to see how scared he was, but she heard him murmur, "Now they can say it's murder."

★ ★ ★

Over breakfast the Whites had almost had a family quarrel, though it was difficult to row in what Jean had aptly termed a 'house under siege'. The quarrel was partly a continuation of the argument that Jean and Greg had had the night before about the presence of yet another policeman in the house, this one manning an extra phone. Jean had refused absolutely to have the man in the kitchen, so that he had been relegated to the utility room.

Now, Jean, Greg and Rosemary sat at the small round table at one end of the kitchen, and tried to keep their voices low. It was shortly before eight. None of them had slept well.

A further point of dissension was what they should do during the day, and how they should cope and behave. Normally, such questions posed few problems, but their present situation was new to them, to say the least.

It was Greg who had precipitated this particular aspect of the argument. He had just told Jean that he had arranged with

Tansey to go into College that morning. He explained that he had to lecture on Milton at ten o'clock, and on Protestant Literature at eleven, and from five to seven that evening he was due to give two tutorials. He saw no reason why the disruption caused by the explosion and the inevitable police inquiries should affect his students, whatever his personal feelings might be.

Jean made no effort to hide her disagreement and disgust. "Get along to your College then, Greg, since you believe your students are more important than we are. Anyway," she added unpleasantly, "you'd better make the most of it. As soon as Sir Philip recovers he'll kick you out of the place!"

"I'm not so sure he can," said Greg, and wondered if planting a bomb under duress in the Master's loo counted as 'reprehensible conduct likely to sully the name of St Xavier's College', as the Statutes put it.

"Just wait!" Jean said softly.

"All right, Jean. And this afternoon I was thinking of going to the hospital, if Tansey will let me. I want to see poor young Fairchild, and I could pay a duty visit to the Master. Perhaps he'll be more understanding than you assume. Meanwhile, when I've had some more coffee, I'll be off to the College."

"And I'll be off to school," said Rosemary.

"Oh no you won't!" Jean was determined on this at least. "Your father may be prepared to face the cameras and reporters lying in wait outside the house — but not you. Have you looked out of the window and seen them?"

"No, but —"

There was a tap at the kitchen door, and one of the police officers who had spent the night in the house poked his head in. "Chief Inspector Tansey wants you on the phone, Mr White, sir."

"Coming."

Greg returned in a very few minutes. His expression was bleak and he made no attempt to soften the blow. "The Senior Tutor died early this morning," he said bluntly. "It was another heart attack, and there's little doubt it was a direct result of that damned explosion."

"Dear God! So now it's become

murder," Jean said, unwittingly echoing Bert Fairchild.

Greg made no attempt to contradict her. Probably for the first time in their married life he was thankful to leave the house and his wife. Ignoring the cameras and the clamouring reporters and the stares of a small group of curious bystanders, he got into the police car on which Tansey had insisted, closed his eyes and tried to make his mind a blank. The drive was over too soon. But the College was not unwelcoming. It was no longer cordoned off, though there was a police officer on duty in the lodge, and everyone going in was questioned and searched.

Dobson greeted Greg with evident pleasure, and in the quad he met Ailsa Mackay carrying a heap of files. The bomb squad had moved out of the Lodgings temporarily, and the debris in the Lodgings had been partially sifted and cleared, so that with the help of a scout Ailsa could move her vital documents and equipment to a room that the Bursar had found for her.

Greg relieved her of the files. He was

concerned for her. She looked ill, her eyes black-circled, her face still distorted by the bruising.

"Ailsa, are you all right? Should you have come in today?"

"I'm fine, Greg, and there's so much to do. Peter Lacque can't manage everything." She hesitated for a moment. "You've heard about Dr Dawson?"

"Yes. The Chief Inspector phoned me."

"He phoned the Bursar too, and now the entire College seems to know — at any rate all the Senior Common Room. Oh, Greg, it makes the whole thing so much worse, doesn't it?"

They had reached the room that was to be Ailsa's temporary office, and she pointed out where to put the files. She waited until the scout had gone, then she turned to Greg. "It's you I'm worried about," she said. "Oh, I know it's not my business. You've got your family and — and so many friends. But in a way it is — my business, I mean — because of the College and because — " She bit her bottom lip to stop herself, terrified at what she had been about to say, and winced as pain shot up her cheekbone. "I'm sorry. I'm being incoherent."

"Yes, I'm afraid you are." Greg took her by the shoulders and gripped tightly. "I'd shake you — " He had nearly said 'kiss you'. "But it might hurt. Ailsa, what's the matter?"

"All these rumours — that you could have warned us but you saved yourself instead, that you actually wanted the Master to be blown up and didn't care about the rest of us, that — that it was you who planted the bomb."

"That's true," Greg said quietly.

"What!"

"I did plant the bomb, Ailsa — but not willingly."

Ailsa listened without interruption as Greg told his story, and it was not until he reached the end that he realized that he had been trying to explain to her the nature of his emotions and just how he had felt, torn between one ghastly alternative and the other. It was not something he had made a great effort to explain even to Jean, he knew, but then he had not expected her to be sensitive or compassionate.

Ailsa offered him no sympathy, but her eyes were full of tears. "Thank you for telling me, Greg. At least now I can set the record straight — and bugger anyone who says anything against you!"

Greg laughed. Ailsa rarely, if ever, used such words. "Let's hope the Master won't be one of them. Jean seems to think he might be."

"She could be right. He and the Senior Tutor were great friends. How — how is Jean, Greg — and Rosemary?"

"Rosemary's been terrific. Jean — Jean's taking it rather hard."

As soon as he had spoken Greg felt that he had been disloyal to his wife. He had no wish to discuss his family with Ailsa, and he was glad that the scout chose that moment to return with another pile of files.

★ ★ ★

Jean was indeed taking it hard, and perhaps she had good reason. Greg had disappeared to St Xavier's, leaving her to cope — as she thought of it — with whatever might arise. Rosemary had retired to her room, saying that, if she weren't allowed to go to school, at least she could do some reading. Jean felt abandoned. On a normal Tuesday she might have done some gardening, gone shopping, written letters — but this was certainly not a normal Tuesday. With three police officers now in the house, including the one manning the phone in the utility room, and others outside, plus the media and the curious onlookers, she felt restless and could settle to nothing.

Lorna Pulent had phoned shortly after Greg had gone to ask if there was anything she could do. She had suggested coffee, lunch, whatever Jean would like or would be useful. Jean had thanked her, but refused her offers. She was fond of Lorna but wasn't prepared to face the inevitable questions. Another friend phoned to commiserate about St Xavier's and, as yet unknowing of the Whites' connection with the disaster, had hoped it wouldn't prevent them coming to dinner the following evening.

The next caller was Tony Pulent, who asked to speak to Rosemary. Rosemary came downstairs willingly enough, and occupied the phone for at least five minutes. She had scarcely put the receiver down when the phone rang again and, thinking that Tony had forgotten something, she picked it up and said, "Hi! What is it, Tony?"

The call was brief. For a minute after it had ended Rosemary leant against the hall table. Her mouth was dry and suddenly, as her mother came out of the sitting-room, she shivered. She was unaware that she had become very pale.

Jean was startled. "Darling, are you all right?"

"Yes. I — I — "

"Rosemary, what's the matter? What did Tony say?"

"It wasn't Tony. I mean, it was Tony the first time. He's coming in later. The other call was — was Tom."

Jean took her by the arm and led her into the sitting-room. "Tell me!" she said fiercely; she hadn't realized that there had been two calls.

Rosemary pulled her arm away. "There isn't much to tell. He said that we needn't worry, Dad had done well enough and they were satisfied."

"Is that all?"

"No. He said that we were to remember to keep our mouths buttoned up, or else — He sounded his nasty, threatening self, as usual."

"I'm sure he did. He's a horror! But let's be thankful they're satisfied in spite of your father doing his best to trick them. It's a great relief."

"If it's true."

"Why shouldn't it be? They've kept their word so far."

Rosemary shrugged. "Yes, I suppose they have. Anyway, I'm going back to my room. I've plenty of work to do. And the chap in the utility room will have heard everything. Tom put his receiver down before I remembered to try to keep him talking."

"That's all right, darling. Forget the police, and let's take care of ourselves."

Rosemary shook her head doubtfully. And when she reached her room she sat for some while at her desk, staring unseeingly at her open book. After Tom had warned that they were to keep their mouths shut he had added, "That goes for you especially, Rosemary, sweetie."

And she knew why.

She wondered what the police would make of it.

* * *

Tony stared at Rosemary in disbelief. He failed to understand. He thought of her not only as attractive, but as intelligent and practical as well; he was proud to have her as his girlfriend, and knew that he was often envied. Most of the time he forgot that she was just sixteen, but that fact had been brought home to him sharply now. He was astonished that she was behaving so stupidly.

"Why on earth didn't you tell your parents — and the Chief Inspector? Don't you realize how important it is that you can identify this guy Tom?"

"But I — I'm not sure I can! I saw his face for a mere second! I'd never be able to pick him out on a — an identity parade."

"You could describe him. You've just described him to me."

"Yes," Rosemary said sulkily.

She kicked at the leg of the chair

on which she was sitting. After Tom's threatening phone call that morning she had needed to tell someone, and Tony had seemed the obvious person. Her father wasn't there and anyhow he had enough problems of his own without extra worry about her. Her mother, she was certain, would either have scorned what she had to say, or have sworn her to silence, probably both. And, like Tony, they would have demanded to know why she hadn't mentioned it before.

"Don't you want these chaps to get caught?" Tony was exasperated.

"Yes, of course, but — "

"But what? You don't sound too sure, Rosemary. Don't you realize that until they're caught your father's going to be under a certain amount of suspicion, After all, it was he who — "

"Shut up! How dare you suggest — " Rosemary sprang to her feet.

"I'm not suggesting anything against Greg. You know I admire him more than anyone I know." Tony was placatory. "But other people may."

Rosemary subsided. "All right! But I've tried to explain. There was never a good moment to admit I'd seen Tom's face — and now Mum will be furious. I think she wants the whole affair to be forgotten as if it never happened. And it's not as if I believed I could identify him."

"Nevertheless, the Chief Inspector *must* be told what you know. It could help enormously." Tony paused. "Rosemary, would you like me to — to tackle Tansey for you?"

"Would you?"

"Of course! Go over it again so I'm sure I've got the facts straight."

Rosemary did her best. There wasn't much — short, sandy hair, blue-grey eyes, reddish face, crooked nose. It could have been the description of countless men.

"And that's all I can tell you, Tony — or the police. I had no more than a brief glimpse — and I was busy at the time — you know what I mean?"

"I know," Tony said gently.

Rosemary suddenly went on. "The only funny thing is I feel certain I've seen Tom — or someone very like him — somewhere before. I'm sure I'm not imagining that."

12

IT was not until the evening of that day, Tuesday, that Detective Chief Inspector Tansey went to make his report to the Chief Constable. In the interval his time had been busy but fruitful, though mostly in a negative sense, or so he then believed. Certainly, he admitted to himself that he had made little positive progress, though he had 'cleared some of the undergrowth', as he put it. He comforted himself with the thought that, at this stage of the case, that was more or less to be expected.

His first task had been to give a formal press conference, at which he provided a sympathetic account of Greg White's action, and repeated his firm belief that the bombing was an attempt at a revenge killing. Then, in company with Detective-Sergeant Abbot, he had set off for the hospital in the hope of interviewing Sir Philip Pinel, the Master of St Xavier's College, whom he had never met. Having dispatched Abbot to interview Fairchild, Tansey found Pinel sitting up in bed in a private room, and thought him an impressive figure, even though his great domed head was swathed in a bandage. It was not until he was to see the Master standing up that Tansey was to revise this opinion; unfortunately, the Master's splendid torso ended in very short legs.

Apart from his appearance when seated, Pinel was in fact not a specially impressive character. He was impatient and irascible; his main concern seemed to be what harm the bombing might cause to the College Fund, as if a fall in such contributions was more important than the death of his friend Dr Dawson, or Fairchild's broken leg or the shock that had been suffered by everyone exposed to the explosion in the Lodgings.

"We're a small College," said the Master. "With costs rocketing as they are, we need all the support we can get, and no one — old St Xavier's man or not — is going to lend his name or give money to a cause that's not reputable. I simply do not understand Mr White. How could he bring himself to plant that infernal weapon? Has the man no sense of duty? When it becomes known that it was one of St Xavier's own senior members who — It's totally disgraceful!"

"Mr White was acting under duress, Sir Philip."

"So he maintains. But why, I ask, should these supposed men have chosen Gregory White as their — their messenger of doom — rather than anyone else?"

Tansey ignored what he assumed to be a rhetorical question. "Can you think of anyone who bears you a grudge, Sir Philip — or St Xavier's?"

"People always bear grudges," said Pinel shortly.

But few, Tansey thought, worked them off in such a violent fashion and, when the Master continued to be unhelpful, he was forced to prompt him by mentioning the thieving scout, the student expelled for drug pushing and the don who — The Chief Inspector got not further with his recital. Sir Philip had gone red in the face and was ringing for his nurse.

"No loyalty!" he stuttered. "Have they no loyalty — telling you these dreadful tales about the College, making the place sound like a den of thieves and whores and drug addicts?"

Thankfully Tansey withdrew from the presence. At the nurse's station he inquired about Lady Pinel, but was told that there had been no need to detain her overnight. Apparently she had gone to stay with her sister and brother-in-law, who lived in Norham Gardens in North Oxford. Tansey decided to forget her, at least for the present. He joined Abbot, who reported that Fairchild had been uncommunicative and, as expected, had produced only confirmatory evidence.

From the hospital the two police officers had driven out to Cowley. Ailsa Mackay had found the name and address of the garage — a small but seemingly perfectly reputable firm — where Harry Batsford was now working. Batsford was not pleased to see Tansey and Abbot when he learnt who they were.

"What do you want?" he demanded aggressively. "I done nothing wrong."

"We'd just like to ask you a few questions," said Tansey, using the time-honoured sentence.

Batsford glared at them. He was a thin, white-faced boy in overalls that were too big for him and, in spite of his attitude, Tansey understood how he could arouse sympathy. He looked a pathetic creature.

"You'd better come into the office then." Batsford led the way into a minute box-like room, decorated like the offices of all small garages with calendars featuring semi-naked girls in glamorous poses. He pointed to two hard chairs and seated himself on the edge of a desk. "Lucky the boss isn't here at the moment or you'd be getting me the sack. He doesn't like coppers."

Although he had been less than welcoming, Batsford was far from reticent. He seemed to have no hesitation in pouring out information. Perhaps he had hopes of getting rid of Tansey and Abbot before his boss returned.

He freely admitted that he had lost his job as a scout at St Xavier's for petty pilfering. It had been just before Christmas and he'd been skint, as he said. "But I didn't take 'alf the things they said I did. That Betty Fergus,

Davies's bint, she claimed I pinched a diamond ring he'd give her, but I never set eyes on it. Nor had she — set eyes on one — I bet. Now, if it had been Amanda Hulton — " He paused ruminatively. "She was a peach, that Amanda, and rich, but I wouldn't have stole from her or Mr Fremont or any of that set. They always treated me right. But they got their degrees and off they went, except for Peregrine Courcey and poor old Steve."

Tansey knew about Courcey. So, "Who was this Steve?" he inquired.

"Steve Sarson? Oh, he wasn't really one of them — a kind of hanger-on, you might say. Me, next term I was moved to another staircase with a ripe lot of sods, treated me like dirt, some of them did."

"So you thought them fair game," said Tansey.

Batsford heaved a theatrical sigh. "OK. I agree. I'm not quarrelling with you. I was wrong, but I paid for it. I lost a good job and I learnt my lesson. I've gone straight since."

"You know you were heard threatening to get your own back on St Xavier's?"

"Oh, that was months before Mr White got me taken on here, and if you think I've anything to do with blowing up the blasted place, forget it. I'm happier doing garage work than being a servant to sods no better than what I am, for all their gowns and airs."

"Where were you yesterday?"

It was Abbot who asked the question, surprising Batsford, though he answered immediately. "Right where I am now," he said. "You can ask my boss, and we had one or two regulars come in. They'll speak for me."

"Fair enough." Tansey stood up. "Mind if we look around before we go."

"Same if I do, ain't it?"

But Batsford showed them around the premises without outward resentment, and indeed with a certain amount of pride. There was no sign of a white van. Abbot suggested that they might fill up with petrol and have the oil checked, a request to which Batsford responded quickly and efficiently. They parted from him on reasonably good terms.

Tansey had been thoughtful as they drove away from Cowley. He didn't doubt that Harry Batsford's alibi was genuine — it would be too simple to check — and probably the young man *was* going straight now. But it was interesting that he would possess all the information required to know when and where the bomb should be placed, and also that he had a good reason for not wanting Gregory White, who had obviously befriended him in his troubles, to be blown up. What's more, Batsford could still be bearing a chip on his shoulder, in spite of what he said and however irrational it might be. In Tansey's experience people were very often irrational.

* * *

They might have gone directly to Abingdon to talk to Emma Watson, the woman don who seemed to have scandalized the hierarchy of St Xavier's, but a call from Headquarters came through on the radio. Mr Tony Pulent had been trying to get in touch with Chief Inspector Tansey; he claimed to have urgent information, but refused to divulge it to anyone else.

Slightly irritated to have his plans changed for what he thought would probably be a waste of time, Tansey had nevertheless directed Abbot to St Xavier's, where Tony had said he would be for the rest of the morning. It was always possible that Pulent had happened on some detail that might prove useful, and a visit to the College would show the authorities that the Chief Inspector was taking the case seriously. Tansey, while not overly ambitious, knew that a good word from the University would do him no harm.

And, in the event, the diversion had proved well worth while. The police now had a description of one of the villains, however vague, and Rosemary might still remember why he had looked familiar to her, though such a resemblance could easily turn out to be coincidental. Tansey was not displeased. He had also had an opportunity to speak to Inspector Carey, and to agree that there was no objection to Greg White visiting the Master and Fairchild in hospital later in the day.

* * *

After a quick lunch Tansey and Abbot had once more set out for Abingdon. He had hesitated about phoning Emma Watson to warn her in advance of his coming, and had decided against such a move. It was term time, and she would almost certainly be at the school, so there was no reason to forgo the element of surprise. On the other hand, he had no wish to cause her undue embarrassment, and therefore gave his name to the maid who answered the front door as Mr Tansey, adding that he and Mr Abbot would wait if that would be more convenient for Miss Watson.

The surprise was theirs, however. When Emma Watson appeared she greeted Tansey as Chief Inspector. "I read the newspapers," she said by way of explanation, "and I listen to the local radio. I take it you've come to see me about this bomb at St Xavier's. I can't imagine any other reason."

Miss Watson was a petite woman, blonde and blue-eyed, with a good complexion and a slightly upturned nose.

She was not pretty in the accepted sense of the word, but there was no doubt that she was attractive. Her black skirt, a modest calf-length, and a demure white blouse accentuated rather than minimized her sexiness, and she was perfectly self-possessed, giving both Tansey and Abbot a small polite smile. She waited for one of them to speak.

Tansey recovered quickly. "We're interviewing everyone who might have felt ill will or malice towards the Master of St Xavier's or the College," he began.

"And I come into that category, of course. I hate that old Puritan bastard, Chief Inspector. I won't pretend I don't. The same goes for many of his colleagues, too."

"Not all of them? What about Mr White?"

Emma Watson gave a wide impish grin. "Greg White's a nice man, too nice for his own good perhaps, but I never had an affair with him, if that's what you mean. Nor with the Bursar, though I think Peter Lacque wouldn't have minded. However, I was involved with another man at the time; he and his wife have since gone out to Australia. If you want details about undergraduates, I had a brief fling with Hugh Fremont, and an even briefer fling — in fact, you could call it a one-night stand — with poor Steve Sarson after Amanda Hulton had let him down. And that's all. I smoked pot a few times, but I never slept with any of the druggies, as was rumoured. I'm afraid my reputation far surpassed my achievements, Chief Inspector."

"I see," said Tansey. "Nevertheless, you were asked to leave the College, Miss Watson, and I gather I'm right in assuming you were unable to find an equivalent position."

"Damned right, Chief Inspector, if you mean I couldn't get a reasonable job. Otherwise I wouldn't be teaching — or trying to — in this crummy second-rate school — and lucky to be here, I suppose, after the rotten reference old Pinel gave me. Incidentally, I had classes all yesterday, so I've a splendid alibi. I can't have been blackmailing Greg White into planting that bomb."

"Someone else might have been acting on your behalf, Miss Watson."

Emma Watson laughed. "Come off it, Chief Inspector. Who? And what for? Money? I haven't got any. Love? I don't rate that sort of devotion." For the first time she sounded bitter. "If you're thinking of the father of my dead child, think again. He departed at a rate of knots and he's since married his childhood sweetheart, or so they tell me. By the way, he had no connection with the College and I've no intention of giving you his name."

"So you can't help us?"

"No!"

Tansey had believed her, but he had suspected that even if she could have helped them she wouldn't. What he had not realized was that inadvertently she, like Harry Batsford, the former scout turned garage hand, had given him a valuable lead. He could hardly be blamed for not recognizing this among the welter of information and misinformation he was receiving, but the delay in following up the point was to lead inevitably to further violence.

★ ★ ★

It had been a long hard day, and Dick Tansey had to smother a yawn as he seated himself across the desk from the Chief Constable. He handed over his typed report, and waited until Midvale had skimmed through it. It was a quirk of the Chief Constable's that, on any important matter, he preferred to read reports in the presence of the author and then ask for them to be supplemented with a less formal oral dissertation, before conducting what was in effect a *viva voce*. Not all his senior officers enjoyed a procedure of this kind, but Tansey had always found it rewarding. However, on this occasion he was glad to see that Midvale had already changed into a black tie, which presumably meant that he had a dinner engagement, and that the session couldn't last too long.

"You've certainly covered a lot of ground in a short space of time, Chief Inspector." Midvale shifted his heavy bulk in his chair. "And I agree with your main thesis. This crime has all the hallmarks of a revenge killing which failed to achieve its ultimate object — thanks to Mr White. No terrorist organization has claimed responsibility for it and, unless evidence to the contrary emerges, I accept that we must seek someone with a grudge."

"We've found several of those already, sir, and there may well be more. For instance, we've barely touched on the drugs scandal that the College suppressed last spring."

Midvale grunted. "There's always a lot of feuding going on in these in-grown societies," he said. "And mixing the sexes hasn't helped; I'm not sure it's not made things worse, in spite of what some claim. But it's not usual for the combatants to resort to such extremely violent measures. Usually they prefer a more subtle approach."

"I wouldn't say this was an unsubtle crime, sir." Tansey felt bound to protest. "It seems to me to have been well planned, and carried out with great efficiency. Whoever organized it knew a great deal about the College and its organization, and must have been in a position to judge the White family's likely reactions."

The Chief Constable nodded. "You

think it was an inside job then, and that Tom and the other chap were hired?"

"The Whites don't believe that, sir, for some reason. They were positive the two men were personally involved." Tansey shrugged. "Of course, they could be quite wrong."

"I suppose their neighbours haven't produced any useful evidence?"

"No, sir. We've made the usual house to house inquiries, but no joy. A woman noticed a white van parked in the road early yesterday morning, but she couldn't give any details, and white vans are two a penny around Oxford. Unluckily for us the Whites live in the sort of neighbourhood where people don't pay much attention to each other's affairs."

Midvale glanced at his watch and raised Tansey's hopes that he was about to end the interview, but the Chief Constable continued. "There were three people who should have been at that meeting, but failed to attend it — Chapman, Beale and White. Have Chapman and Beale been checked yet?"

"Yes, it's in the report, sir. Mr Beale has a high temperature. There's no doubt he's genuinely ill. The police officer who went to their house met the doctor. As for Mr Chapman, his injuries are genuine too. I suppose that if he'd known about the explosion he could have fallen off that ladder on purpose in order to avoid the meeting, but the idea seems a bit far-fetched."

"Which leaves us with Mr White." The Chief Constable referred to his watch again, and this time got to his feet. "I'm afraid I must be off. I've a dinner date. We'll talk later in the week, Chief Inspector — or earlier if you think it would help. Meanwhile, I've one suggestion. Try to find out why White was picked. Was it just because he was suitable, a good subject with his wife and daughter to be threatened, or was it because the villains had some reason to like him?"

"Yes, sir," said Tansey dutifully, though at the time he failed to appreciate the importance of the Chief Constable's suggestion.

13

FOR Greg White the next couple of days were among the worst he had ever experienced in his married life. Jean dusted and vacuumed in a state of barely suppressed fury; her cleaning woman had telephoned to say that she was unwell and could not come that week, an excuse Jean scorned. She cooked meals and made polite conversation with her husband and daughter, but she remained aloof, and disdained to show either of them any affection, complaining at intervals about the continuing presence of the police in and around the house. Greg had given up trying to win her over.

Rosemary was only a trifle more responsive. Jean had forbidden her to leave the house, and she sulked, spending most of her time in her room on the grounds that she needed to keep up with her school work as much as she could. Only Tony's visits seemed to rouse her from this lethargic pose.

In the circumstances Greg couldn't be blamed for taking refuge in the College, where he was also safe from the attentions of the media. Although Tansey had done his best to state Greg's case in the most favourable light, the popular tabloids had not been kind to him. That their attitude was largely based on a statement issued by the Master from his hospital bed only made the situation worse. Sir Philip Pinel, without quite putting the point in so many words, had effectively accused Greg of cowardice, and a failure to do his duty to his colleagues and the College.

Greg had been appalled by this attack. Certainly, the Master had been cold and unfriendly when he had visited him in hospital the day after the explosion, but he had not seemed so alarmingly hostile, and the press reports had come as a surprise. What was more, these same reports had tended to complicate still further Greg's relationship with his wife.

Even safe within the College Greg felt something of a pariah. It was not that anyone was positively antagonistic, though he wondered if this atmosphere might change when the Master returned to his duties. But sometimes a silence would fall when he entered the Senior Common Room; groups in the quads or the passages would mysteriously dissolve when he approached; and he was not asked to join the small committee formed to arrange a memorial service for the Senior Tutor.

By Friday Greg found himself keeping to his rooms, and emerging only when it was strictly essential. But he didn't lack visitors. Ailsa Mackay was the most frequent; she came without excuse and Greg was always glad to see her. Peter Lacque, the Bursar, busy as he was, also made a point of looking in. And there were others, though not many, both dons and undergraduates, who were prepared to show their continued affection for and trust in him.

As noon — the time for his last scheduled lecture of the week — drew near, Greg was toying with the idea of finding some pretext or other to cancel it. Neither the subject nor the hour made it popular, and he expected a poor attendance. Suddenly it all seemed a waste of time. The Bursar had just informed him that the Master would be returning to St Xavier's on Monday; he would be unable to use the Lodgings and would be staying with his wife's sister and brother-in-law in Norham Gardens, but he would require a suite of rooms in College. For Greg this was dispiriting news.

"I've heard," he said, as Ailsa came in a little later.

"Heard what? Oh, you mean about the Master? He's going to have the Senior Tutor's rooms." She laughed. "What with the Lodgings out of commission and the police usurping so much space we're getting positively crowded."

"I'm surprised no one's suggested I should move out." Greg was bitter. "Or is Pinel to have that privilege himself?"

"Don't be an idiot, Greg!" Ailsa spoke sharply. "I know things are bad for you at the moment, but they'll get better."

"They could scarcely get worse," Greg replied resentfully.

Ailsa ignored the remark. "Anyhow, that's not what I had to tell you. I went to the hospital yesterday evening to visit

Bert Fairchild. Physically he's doing fine, but mentally he seems in a bad way. He'd hardly speak to me. I gather from the nurse he was no problem to begin with, but now he's suddenly become sunk in gloom. He doesn't want to eat or talk or do anything."

"How odd! I looked in on him when I was at the hospital on Tuesday, but he seemed to be asleep and I didn't disturb him."

"You wouldn't try again, would you?"

"Wouldn't Margaret Sandown be better, or Hugh Fremont if he's at home and not gone back to London? They're the ones who took his old mother to see him, and — "

"Greg, Margaret's a very junior don. At the time she was available, and as she's a sensible girl and Hugh volunteered to drive them, it was the best solution. Peter Lacque has been to see him since, but Fairchild wouldn't talk to him either."

"What makes you think he'd be any more likely to talk to me?"

"Perhaps he won't, but — "

"But you consider it's my duty as I'm responsible for him being in hospital?"

The clock on the mantel struck twelve. "Good Heavens! Ailsa, I must fly. I'm due to lecture. Too late to cancel it now." He struggled into his gown and collected his books and notes. "All right. I'll pay young Fairchild a visit this afternoon. I might as well make use of my chauffeur-driven police car."

"Thanks, Greg. Bless you!"

Feeling inexplicably more cheerful after this conversation with Ailsa, Greg ran down the staircase and hurried through the archway into the second quad. He was slightly out of breath as he reached the lecture hall, and he paused to calm himself. There wasn't a sound from within, and he decided that if there were fewer than a dozen students he would send them away.

He opened the door, took two or three steps into the hall, and stopped. The place was packed. As he walked slowly towards the platform, climbed the three or four stairs to it and placed his books and papers on the table in front of him the audience rose to its feet and started to clap. Even when he held up a hand in an attempt to end the demonstration the clapping continued, steadily and rhythmically. For a brief moment Greg was convinced that this was a hostile slow hand-clap, but the expressions on the smiling faces of those before him quickly disabused him of this idea. Clearly, they were on his side.

He waited — there was nothing else he could do — and while he waited he scanned the audience. Many were his own students. Some, such as Tony Pulent, he knew socially. Some he had noticed about the College, though he couldn't put a name to them. Yet others were a surprise. What were Hugh Fremont and Amanda Hulton doing there, seated on either side of Peregrine Courcey? They had both graduated the summer before last, and had no reason to attend his lecture.

Suddenly, as if at a given signal, the clapping stopped and there was a scurry of noise as they all resumed their seats. Greg realized that he must make some suitable reply, though he found it difficult to choose the right words.

"For the life of me I — I can't think

why I should have deserved that," he began.

"It was a vote of confidence," shouted a voice from the back of the hall.

"Well, thank you — thank you very much. Believe me, I appreciate it. My morale's not exactly high at the moment, and that reception's given it a great boost." He paused. "And now I'm about to deliver a normal lecture so, if any of you would like to depart, I'd quite understand."

No one moved. He gave them a minute, then started to talk about the effect of Milton's religious beliefs on the poet's work. They listened, though it was not the most inspired of lectures. There was very little fidgeting. Some individuals even took notes. He had never had such a large and attentive audience before, but his voice was hoarse and he was glad to bring his discourse to an end after some three-quarters of an hour.

Hurriedly scooping up his books and papers, he said, "Thank you again, everyone." He gave a wave of his hand and escaped from the hall. He was touched. After that reception, he thought, if the authorities tried to get rid of him he would fight. He would do his utmost to remain at St Xavier's.

* * *

If the last two days had been depressing for Greg White and his family, they had been frustrating for Detective Chief Inspector Tansey. A lot of officers had done a lot of work on his behalf, but the results had been meagre in the extreme. To put it bluntly, the investigation had made no progress.

Tansey, concentrating on the 'grudge' theory, as he had come to call it, had interviewed the young man who had been sent down from St Xavier's and was at present in jail, but he found no reason to connect him in any way with the explosion at the College. The same was true of his former girlfriend, and of the other 'druggies' whom the Master had treated more leniently.

Tansey had also given serious consideration to the proposition suggested by the Chief Constable, that the choice of Greg White to plant the bomb might have some special significance, but the Chief Inspector had found no evidence to support — or, for that matter, deny — his superior's suggestion. White was not the only St Xavier's don with access to the meeting who held hostages to fortune. Chapman, Beale and Mead were all married. Chapman — the man who had fallen off his ladder — had three small children; Beale had a teenage son; Mead had a son and a daughter. And, as far as Tansey could judge, they were all reasonably popular characters. Yet Greg White had been preferred by the villains, who had nevertheless seemed to stress the fact that they wished him and his family no direct harm.

"Of course, there could easily be someone we've not heard of, someone who's been cherishing resentment against the Master and the College in secret." Tansey was in a ruminative mood.

"You mean from way back, sir?" said Abbot.

It was the tail end of Friday, and the two detectives were in the Chief Inspector's office in Kidlington. Tansey, with promptings from Abbot, had been trying to sum up progress with the case so far. It was this attempt which had caused his frustration.

"Possibly," he replied. "To date we've only considered the last academic year. Whatever occasioned this malice could have been rumbling on over a long period, but it's got to be something important — unless we're dealing with a crazy villain. No one's going to blow up the Master and his senior colleagues because they weren't invited to a party, say!"

"There's another point too, sir. This bomb. I know you can learn how to make one from books, though it must be jolly risky, but the forensic boys say it was comparatively sophisticated, and it must have taken time to assemble the ingredients and construct it. Maybe that could account for any delay."

"Yes. That idea — anyone trying to purchase suitable materials and so on — is being looked into, as you know. But no joy up till now."

The telephone rang, and Abbot answered. "Mr White wants to see you urgently, sir. He's at the College, but if it's convenient for you he'd prefer to come by here before he goes home."

Tansey hesitated. It was already after seven. Hilary would have put the baby to bed, and would be wondering whether to have supper by herself or wait for him. "All right. Tell Mr White that'll be fine". But he had seen the shadow pass across Abbot's face as he put down the receiver, and he added, "No need for you to stay, Bill."

"Thanks, sir!"

Tansey grinned at him. He didn't mind some time to himself. He called his wife to say he would be late, thankful that as a former detective-sergeant she was understanding, and he concentrated on the paperwork in his in-tray until Greg White was announced.

"I'm sorry to keep you, Chief Inspector, but I was some time at the hospital and then I had tutorials."

Tansey waved him to a chair, "You've been to the hospital again?"

"Yes. Ailsa — Miss Mackay — suggested that I should visit young Fairchild. She said he was down in the dumps and perhaps I could cheer him up — you

218

could argue it's my fault he's there at all, at least that's how I reasoned, but I wasn't altogether right."

"Mr White, I'm sorry, but you're not being very clear."

"No, I'm not, am I?" Greg gave a rueful grin. What with lack of sleep and general strain he was not feeling at his brightest. "Let me try again. This afternoon, after talking to Miss Mackay, I went to the hospital to see Bert Fairchild. I felt some responsibility for him. I didn't really think I could help him, but I was wrong. He was worried and scared and by the time I got there I found he'd been wanting to talk to someone. He believed I'd understand and would help him, because I was involved in this bomb business too. So he chose me as his father confessor."

"People seem to make a habit of picking you to help them, Mr White."

"I wish to God they didn't."

Tansey laughed. Then, suddenly serious, he said, "So what did Fairchild have to confess?"

"As he told it, it was a lengthy story. I'll try to keep it brief. Fairchild rides a bicycle, but he yearns for a motorbike, and he's saving up for one — a powerful and pretty expensive Yamaha, I gather — so he needs money. This summer he was knocked off his bicycle by a white van. The driver blamed himself for carelessness and was full of apologies. He insisted on taking Fairchild to a nearby pub, where he learnt all about the motorbike. He said he might be able to put some cash in Fairchild's way, and they arranged to meet again.

"When they did, this chap asked Fairchild a lot of curious questions, about his job, where in the College he could go, how the Master lived, if he still had meetings of the tutors in the Lodgings, and who went to them." Greg stopped as he sensed Tansey's quickened interest.

"Are you sure about those last questions? They suggest the chap had some knowledge of the College."

"Fairchild seemed sure. Of course, you'll have to talk to him yourself, but I questioned him carefully. He admits he got a bit drunk and can't remember all he was asked, but he's positive about those points. And he's not stupid, Chief Inspector."

"Go on."

"There's not much more. The chap said he was sorry, but the job he'd had in mind for Fairchild had fallen through. He gave Fairchild twenty pounds — compensation for the bicycle accident he called it — and Fairchild's never seen him since. I'd guess he felt uneasy about the incident for a while, and then forgot it until the explosion — and especially the death of Dr Dawson, which seems to have bothered him. As I said, he's not stupid, and he's an honest enough boy, so that once he put two and two together his conscience has been bothering him."

"Did he give any description of his benefactor?"

"Fairly tall and thin. He wore jeans and a leather jacket, and the sort of peaked cap that painters wear. It covered his hair, but his eyebrows were very black. He had tinted glasses, a reddish face and a crooked nose. It's not a bad description, is it?"

"No, indeed not," said Tansey thought-fully. "Mr White, between ourselves for the moment, has your daughter ever told you that she saw Tom's face?"

"No, by God, she hasn't! How could she?"

"It was when she was struggling with him on the bathroom floor. She pulled his hood off." Tansey paused, then went on, "Mr White, you mustn't think I'm intruding, but naturally I know something about the situation in your household. I imagine Rosemary was half afraid to admit she could identify one of the villains in case her mother became even more upset. Anyway, she told Tony Pulent, who told me. I've not spoken to her myself yet, but now I'll have to. Her description ties up reasonably well with Fairchild's description of the man in the pub. Many thanks for your intervention. I'm most grateful to you."

"I see," said Greg. "You may well be right — about Rosemary's attitude, I mean. But I'm glad she had enough sense to come clean, if only indirectly."

"So am I," said Tansey. "Now, is there

anything else? Any ideas of your own on the matter?"

Greg shook his head. "Not really. I'm still convinced that Tom and the man he call 'Boss' were personally involved, and not bribed or hired by anyone else, and I've wondered — "

"Yes — " Tansey prompted.

"It may sound snobbish, but they didn't sound to me as having ever been university material, as it were, and if one of them had been a scout or a member of the quite large staff that keeps the College running and in good repair they wouldn't have needed to ask all those questions about the Master and the Lodgings. I know this seems to contradict the idea that they were personally involved, unless — and this is just a vague thought — unless they were trying to — to avenge someone close to them, a brother perhaps, who *had* been at the College in some capacity."

Tansey appreciated the argument, but he also saw its weakness. The villains wouldn't have needed to cross-question Fairchild if the individual they were avenging was available. The Chief

Inspector nearly raised this point, but he was sorry for Greg White who, tired and unhappy as he obviously was, nevertheless had done his best to be helpful. Tansey let the moment pass. It was a mistake he was to regret.

14

THE week that followed was uneventful. Life at St Xavier's quickly reverted to near-normality. True, there was still a police presence in the College, but it was no longer obtrusive. Inspector Carey continued to occupy the set of rooms he shared with Chief Inspector Tansey, but his staff had been cut and there was now only one officer on duty in the lodge. The Master had returned. Each day he sorrowfully inspected the Lodgings, where progress was slow; the hammering and banging as renovation began was a constant which most people came to ignore, though the dust that was raised didn't help the Bursar's asthma. The media, temporarily at least, seemed to have lost interest.

The White household had also returned to comparative normalcy. Greg now drove himself into central Oxford or caught a bus. At the College he lectured and gave tutorials and went about his usual business; he avoided the Master as much as possible. Rosemary was once more back at school, and was not displeased to find herself the centre of attraction. For her part, Jean was thankful to be rid of police in the house. There had been no more telephone calls from Tom, and the obscene calls from strangers that unpleasant publicity always seems to bring in its wake had ceased. To an extent she too had resumed her customary routine, though her relations with Greg were still strained and she remained angry with Rosemary for not having admitted earlier that she had glimpsed Tom's face.

As for Tansey, he was far from happy with the situation, but there was nothing he could do about it. He had insisted on a round the clock watch over the Whites' house, but there was no surveillance on them as individuals. He regretted this. He was especially fearful for Rosemary in case Tom believed she could identify him, but he accepted that it was impossible to offer her personal protection. For one thing, there had been a large number of influenza cases throughout the Thames

Valley, and the police, hit badly, had even less staff available than usual.

Nor was Tansey pleased with the way the case was progressing, or rather failing to progress. Forced to carry the workload of a sick colleague, he had been unable to give it as much time and attention as he would have wished. But by dint of working long hours he had managed to interview more members of the College, both academic and other staff, and to study the many reports that had continued to pour in. Unfortunately, none of this effort was helpful, and he had to tell the Chief Constable that he was getting nowhere.

"I suppose you've considered getting the girl to help make a photofit of this man Tom, and distributing it to the local forces, Chief Inspector?" Midvale asked tentatively.

"Of course, sir. But I've been hesitating because I was afraid that too wide a distribution would put Rosemary White at greater risk. I suspect Tom would guess she was the main source; he can't believe that Fairchild's description would be of much use to us by itself. There's another point too, sir. I've never had much luck with photofits, and I've been wondering whether something a bit less mechanical and formalized might appeal to the girl and get more out of her. In other words — Stanhope."

Stanhope was a local artist sometimes employed by the Thames Valley police. "I take your point," said the Chief Constable. "Very well. Let's try him first."

"As a matter of fact, I've already organized a session, sir. For tomorrow morning. As it's a Saturday Rosemary won't be at school so it can be done without a fuss."

"Good idea," said Midvale.

★ ★ ★

Rosemary arrived at the Headquarters of the Thames Valley Force at ten o'clock the next morning. She was accompanied not by her mother, as Tansey had feared, but by Tony Pulent. Sergeant Abbot met them in the reception hall and took them along to Tansey's office, where they were introduced to Robert Stanhope.

Stanhope had set up an easel with a thick pad of paper. He explained to them how he started — with a round, an oval or a square — to represent the approximate shape of the face. Then, as Rosemary filled in the details the portrait could take shape. It was essential that Rosemary should advise him and correct him so that eventually a likeness of the man she knew as Tom might emerge.

"It's a rather demanding exercise, I'm afraid," he said, smiling at Rosemary, "but it's interesting, and everything depends on you. Don't hesitate to tell me if I go wrong. I'll just flick over to the next sheet and we'll try again."

Rosemary returned his smile. She hadn't expected the artist to be so young and attractive. Stanhope was in his late twenties, dark-haired, blue-eyed and fully aware of his charm.

"I'll do my best," she said, and added, "I saw him — Tom, I mean — last night."

Tansey and Abbot were astounded, but Stanhope spoke first, "What? But that's great!"

"She thinks she saw him," Tony said,

addressing Tansey. He had taken an instinctive dislike to Stanhope. "It was probably imagination."

"I tell you, I saw him! And he saw me!" Rosemary didn't enjoy being contradicted.

"Where and when?" Tansey intervened.

"Outside the Apollo Theatre, yesterday evening. We were queuing for tickets and he passed on the pavement. I could almost have touched him. He stared directly at me as he went under a street lamp, and I saw his expression change. I did *not* imagine it. I recognized him, and he recognized me."

"Well," said Tansey, "that suggests he may be a local man, which could help to narrow the search. Incidentally, Miss White, you said before that Tom reminded you of someone. You've not yet remembered who, have you?"

"No. It niggles at me, but I don't get anywhere."

"Probably some pop singer," Tony grunted.

Rosemary threw him a glance of disgust, and turned to Stanhope. "Tom has a round face," she began, "and a crooked nose . . . ”

Stanhope drew charcoal sketch after charcoal sketch, making minute revisions as Rosemary instructed him. Tony, in spite of his irritation with her, was fascinated by the growth of the portrait. At last Rosemary slowly shook her head.

“It’s not quite right,” she said, “but I don’t know why. Colour might help.”

“Of course,” Stanhope agreed at once. “Give me about twenty minutes.”

“What about coffee in the meantime,” Tansey suggested. He took them along to the officers’ mess and brought coffee and pastries from the bar. On a Saturday morning the place was three-quarters empty. Tony chatted about St Xavier’s and told Tansey of the surprise ovation that Greg White had received.

“He never said anything at home,” Rosemary remarked. “I didn’t know about it till Tony told me.”

“He deserved it,” said Tony. “He’s a great man, Chief Inspector. For his sake you’ve got to clear up this business. It’ll be a crying shame if he’s forced to leave the College because of it.”

"Is that likely?"

"The Master's got it in for him all right, and Pinel's a pretty powerful figure."

They were interrupted by Stanhope, who declared he was finished and led the way back to Tansey's office. He had arranged the easel so that the portrait faced them as they came through the door. Rosemary gasped when she saw it.

"That's wonderful," she exclaimed at once. "It *is* Tom. You've made his hair a bit too red, but otherwise it's as I remember him. Mind you, I only saw him for a second or two, but — but it wasn't a moment I'll forget easily. And I wasn't wrong, Tony. It *was* Tom I saw yesterday evening."

Tony didn't answer immediately. He was frowning at the picture. At last he said, "Extraordinary! Absolutely extraordinary!"

"What is it?" Rosemary demanded.

"I know whom he reminds you of. It's poor old Steve. Steve Sarson."

"Steve? Yes. So it does. That's right. How silly!" Rosemary sat back in what was not a comfortable chair. "I'm sorry, Chief Inspector."

Tansey knew that he had come across
the name before, but rather than search
the files he asked, "Who's Steve Sarson?"

Tony answered. "Steve was up at
St Xavier's. He was two years ahead of
me, the same year as Hugh Fremont. He
was a scholar and pretty bright. Everyone
expected him to get a First."

"And he didn't?"

"I honestly don't know, but somehow
I rather doubt it. He didn't seem to do
much work in his last year."

"Dad would know," Rosemary said.
"Steve was a pupil of his. That's how I
came to meet him. At one time he used
to come to the house for tutorials or extra
coaching, and he was occasionally invited
to the supper parties that Mum gives. But
does it matter, Chief Inspector? Surely
it must be just chance that there was
a resemblance between Steve and that
horrid Tom."

"Was?" asked Tansey. "What's happened to Steve?"

"He's dead. He was drowned in the
Cherwell the summer before last."

"An accident?"

"No. He committed suicide," Tony

said. "Everyone was horrified, especially Amanda — Amanda Hulton. She blamed herself, but in a way it was as much Hugh Fremont's fault or Peregrine Courcey's. They didn't bother to keep in touch with him. Steve was a nice guy, quiet and clever and he should have got his First and gone on to be an academic somewhere. That's what he wanted." Tony was having difficulty in explaining.

"But — " Tansey encouraged.

"For some reason in his last year he was moved to a different staircase. Among others Hugh and Peregrine had rooms there, and through them Steve met Amanda. The three of them 'took him up', as people used to say. But he was never really one of them. He had no money; he'd come from a comprehensive school and was dependent on his scholarships and grants. His background was quite different from theirs. He'd never been abroad or done any of the things they'd done. They were a pretty high-powered lot, you know, and you could say he didn't speak the same language. Then of course, to make matters worse, he fell head over heels in love with Amanda."

By now Tansey had remembered where he had heard the name of Steve Sarson. The one-time scout, Harry Batsford, had mentioned him in connection with Amanda Hulton, and the sexy Emma Watson had said she'd had a 'one-night stand' with him.

"I assume Amanda jilted him," Tansey said.

"Jilted? That's an old-fashioned word, Chief Inspector. But no, she didn't jilt him. She simply never considered him in that light, and I'm sure she made it perfectly clear." Tony shrugged. "You can't blame her — or him, but it's a pity it should have happened that way."

"Poor old Steve," Rosemary said. "It was no reason for him to drown himself." She studied the portrait on the easel. "It's strange — creepy — that he should be so like Tom. Of course Steve's nose was straight and he was younger and more — more innocent-looking."

"Perhaps they were related." Tansey voiced his thoughts and was at once aware that the remark sounded feeble. He smiled apologetically. "But even if they'd been brothers, Tom would scarcely have tried to avenge Steve's death by bombing St Xavier's and the Master, would he? The target would surely have been this Amanda Hulton."

"So the picture's been no use?" Rosemary was disappointed.

"It most certainly has," Tansey assured her. "We'll circulate it — though not publicly — and with luck an officer will recognize Tom, or spot him in the street as you say you did. Then we'll make some inquiries and when we're sure it *is* Tom, we'll try and trace his companion, put a case together and charge them."

"How simple you made it sound, sir," said Sergeant Abbot when Stanhope had packed up his possessions and departed with Rosemary and Tony.

"I wish it were. It seems to me to get more and more complex. Why did this chap Sarson, who seems to bear a strong resemblance to one of the villains, have to have some connection with St Xavier's College? Why couldn't he have been at some other college — or preferably at Cambridge? It's too much of a coincidence, Bill, and I don't like coincidences."

Officially neither the Chief Inspector nor Sergeant Abbot were on duty that afternoon, but because it was a lovely day, because his wife's sister had come to spend the weekend and he knew they would enjoy a good gossip together, because he was restless — and because he disliked coincidences, Tansey decided to pay a sudden call on Amanda Hulton.

He knew that the Hultons lived in the Cotswolds, and he got the address from St Xavier's. That Amanda Hulton would not be there was a chance he was prepared to take; Ailsa Mackay had told him that Amanda was at present working at home on a biography of one of her ancestors, but it was unlikely that she would be occupied with it on a beautiful Saturday afternoon.

Tansey didn't bother to recall Abbot and drove himself at a leisurely pace. The sky was a pale grey-blue, the leaves already in their autumnal colours, the rolling Oxfordshire hills looking their best, and once he was off the main road there was very little traffic. He stopped

237

in the market town of Colombury to ask the way. Even so he passed the entrance to the Hultons' place and had to turn back.

The house was called Broadlands and, from all he had heard of Amanda Hulton, he had expected it to be of a fair size. But he had not expected the Palladian-style mansion that confronted him at the end of a long drive bordered by lime trees. A white-coated houseman opened the door to him and, once he had identified himself and explained his errand, showed him into a rather large and formidable book-lined room.

It was some minutes before an extremely pretty girl appeared. She was tall and slim, with long fair hair pulled severely back from her face and held at the nape of her neck by a black bow. She wore black slacks and a long-sleeved sweater which Tansey assumed was made of cashmere. She was completely self-possessed, although her colour was high.

"Good afternoon, Chief Inspector. I'm Amanda Hulton. I can't imagine why you should want to talk to me, but come along to my sitting-room. It's more comfortable than the library."

She led the way across the hall and along a corridor, then stood aside to allow Tansey to go into the room ahead of her. It was, as she had said, more comfortable than the library. The furnishings were modern, and there were bright modern paintings on the walls. But he scarcely had time to appreciate it.

Hugh Fremont rose to greet him, hand outstretched. "Hello, Chief Inspector, I didn't expect to meet you here."

"That goes for me too, Mr Fremont," Tansey refused to be disconcerted.

Amanda waved him to a chair and sat herself on a sofa next to Hugh. They held hands. They smiled at Tansey, who was in no hurry to start the conversation. He waited.

Hugh gave a deprecatory gesture. "You must be the first to congratulate us, Chief Inspector. We've just got engaged."

"Really? Then I do congratulate you, and I apologize for having intruded at such an inappropriate time."

"That's not important, Chief Inspector," said Amanda. "But why have you come? It's over a year since I graduated from

St Xavier's, so it can't be about the explosion there."

"I've come primarily to ask what you can tell me about Steve Sarson," Tansey said.

"Oh no." A shadow passed over Amanda Hulton's face. "Steve? Not that again! I hoped that business was all over."

"Steve's dead, Chief Inspector," put in Hugh Fremont. "He drowned himself in the Cherwell. There's no doubt it was suicide. He left a note saying he was so unhappy he no longer wanted to live. You can find it all in your files, I'm sure." Hugh sighed. "Of course, we were horrified. We felt that if we'd realized we might have saved him, and we blamed ourselves."

"Rightly, too," Amanda said. "He was almost penniless by our standards — his father was a carpenter or a plumber or something like that — and we treated him as — as a kind of pet. We took him to restaurants and the theatre and dances, and to London, to nightclubs. We took him racing. We gave him expensive presents on his birthday. Then it was time for Finals, and we couldn't have made it more clear that this was goodbye. He wasn't going to be part of our future."

"And you believe that was why he took his own life?" Tansey asked, thinking that she had provided a useful gloss on what Tony Pulent had already told him.

"Why are you raking up this old dirt now, Chief Inspector?" Hugh sounded suddenly indignant.

"Because I need to know, Mr Fremont," Tansey replied curtly.

"Hugh, it doesn't matter. If we don't tell him someone else will." Amanda released her hand from Hugh's and sighed. "Steve asked me to marry him. It was a — a preposterous idea, and I refused. Probably I was less kind than I might have been, but he took me by surprise. I'd never encouraged him, though it was suggested at the inquest that I had."

"Did you ever receive any threats after Steve was drowned, Miss Hulton?"

Amanda looked surprised. "Threats, Chief Inspector? No! Why do you ask that?"

"You did imply that someone thought

you might have been to blame for his death."

"Oh, you mean — But that was my tutor, Dr Dawson."

"The one who's just died?"

"Yes. The Master was unwell and poor old Harold stood in for him at the inquest."

"It would have made more sense if it had been Greg White who had blamed Amanda and the rest of us," Hugh intervened. "Steve was his pupil, not Dawson's, and it's true we stopped Steve working as hard as he should have done if he was to get a First."

"What sort of degree did he get?"

It was an idle question. Tansey had decided that he had learnt all he was likely to get from the present interview. Hugh and Amanda exchanged glances and together shook their heads.

"I don't know," Hugh said. "Probably a Third. Certainly not a First. In any case, he was dead by the time the Honours Lists were published."

It was a pathetic obituary, Tansey thought as he drove back to Oxford. They hadn't really cared a damn about

Steve Sarson. Amanda had admitted it. They hadn't even bothered to look for his name in the examination results. Not out of malice but from pure thoughtlessness they had tempted Steve with a way of life he could only envy, and he had not been strong enough, mentally or physically, to resist the temptation. But this tragedy — and it *was* a minor tragedy — had happened over a year ago. There had been no threats then and, if someone had taken his time to avenge Steve, why had he attacked the Master and the senior members of St Xavier's, who could scarcely be held personally responsible? The idea made no sense at all.

15

WHILE Chief Inspector Tansey was driving through the Cotswold lanes on his way home, Rosemary White was playing tennis. She had cycled a couple of miles to a friend's house, and had already played two strenuous sets of singles, winning one and losing one. It was now three-all in the third set, and she was determined to win. She was enjoying her afternoon.

Eventually, after a great struggle she did win the final set. She accepted a glass of lemonade, but refused to stay for tea. Her friend's mother had returned, and Rosemary had no wish to face a barrage of questions about the explosion at St Xavier's College and the White family's involvement with it.

"Thank you," she said politely, "but I ought to get back. Mum's visiting a neighbour who's sick, and Dad's alone."

They didn't try to keep her. Rosemary

mounted her bicycle and set off for home. What with the morning spent at police headquarters and winning the match that afternoon she decided it had been a satisfactory day. It was not until she was turning into her own road that she became aware of a white van behind her.

For a moment she panicked, but she could see her house and the policeman lounging against the low wall in front of it. He straightened as he saw her coming towards him. She kept close to the side of the road and pedalled fast. The van overtook her, then without warning swerved right in front of her, braked hard to a full stop and immediately accelerated away.

Rosemary had no chance. She rode straight into the rear of the van as it stopped, hitting it with considerable force. Her front wheel buckled and the bike slithered sideways. The effect on Rosemary was the same as if she had been riding a horse that had refused at the last moment to take a fence. She was flung out of her saddle, described a parabola in the air and landed on the pavement. She was lucky not to have hit her head on the van.

She lay, stunned. Momentarily she blacked out, but she had regained consciousness by the time the police officer had reached her. He was kneeling beside her, choking back his curses, as she opened her eyes.

A passing car stopped and the driver got out. A pedestrian hurried across the road. The owner of the house opposite, who had been looking out of the window and seen what had happened, came to offer help. They were all witnesses, but no one — not even the officer — had had the sense to note the number of the van, and they couldn't agree as to whether it had been an accident or a deliberate attempt to maim, if not kill. Rosemary herself had no doubt, but her one desire was to make light of the incident.

"Get me home!" she ordered the policeman.

He helped her to her feet. There was a gash down her leg, which was bleeding, and she felt bruised and shaken, but no bones seemed to be broken. She was able to walk, though her ankle hurt her and she leant heavily on the officer as they went slowly towards her house. The neighbour and the passer-by came behind them, carrying her damaged bicycle and her tennis racket and shoes.

Greg opened the door. "Dear God!" he said when he saw the little procession. "Darling, what's happened?"

At the sight of her father, Rosemary's courage finally deserted her. "Dad! Oh Dad!" she sobbed, and flung herself into his outstretched arms.

* * *

Tansey heard the news on his radio phone as he approached north Oxford and drove straight to the Whites' home. He spoke briefly to the police officer and was about to ring the bell when the door opened. It was Greg showing out the doctor.

The Chief Inspector waited until the doctor had reached his car. Then, "How is she, Mr White?" he demanded without preamble.

"You know what happened?" asked Greg.

"Oh yes," said Tansey. "I've heard all the details — or as many as my wretched man was able to give me. I'll put an extra officer on duty for a few days."

"Fine," said Greg. "As far as Rosemary's concerned, she's not too bad, thank heavens! She's got a nasty cut on her leg, a sprained ankle and a few bruises. I think the worst thing is probably the shock. Do you have to see her? She's resting. The doctor gave her a mild sedative."

"No, I don't need to see her now. I just wanted to make sure she was — all right."

"Kind of you. Come in." Greg led the way to his study. "My wife's out, which is lucky. She's pretty tense at present, understandably — and this isn't going to help."

"I'm sorry."

Greg nodded. "It's a bloody business," he said with a sudden spurt of anger. "If only they hadn't chosen me."

"Then you might be in hospital — or dead."

"I realize that. Nevertheless, I find it hard to count my blessings, especially after this — this attack on Rosemary. Chief Inspector, tell me honestly, are you managing to get anywhere with the case?"

Tansey hesitated; he didn't want to raise too many false hopes, but finally he said, "I think so, yes. Did Rosemary tell you that she thinks she saw the man we know as Tom last night, and that he saw her? That could be important. For one thing, it would explain the attack on her today. She'd only seen him fleetingly before, and he may have thought he was safe. But if she showed some signs of recognition — well, he knows she can identify him. And indeed it would seem she might, because, as you know, this morning she helped a police artist to produce what she claimed was an excellent likeness. Incidentally, Mr White, she said it reminded her of your old student Steve Sarson. What was more, Tony Pulent — who was with her — agreed."

"Steve! Steve Sarson! But he's dead."

"Quite. I know. I was talking to Amanda Hulton and Hugh Fremont earlier this afternoon. Steve Sarson,

I gather, committed suicide because Miss Hulton had scorned his proposal of marriage, and she and her friends made it clear that once they'd gone down from the university they didn't expect to continue with what Sarson had assumed would be a close and enduring friendship. Would you agree with all that, Mr White?"

"From what I know of the situation, I couldn't disagree, though I wouldn't have put it quite so brutally."

"But did his suicide surprise you? What sort of man was Steve Sarson?"

Greg White gave the Chief Inspector a long stare. "Yes, it did surprise me. Certainly, he'd been bowled over by Amanda Hulton. He'd been entranced by a way of life to which he was not accustomed. But he wasn't an innocent. He was used to fighting for what he wanted, or with his background he'd have had more difficulty in winning a place at Oxford. After a short 'down', I'd have expected him to get a grip on himself and say, 'OK, I'll show you. I'll get to the top, and then — ' It might have been a pipe-dream and come to nothing, but in my opinion he was the kind of chap who'd have tried."

"That's most interesting. But what about this short 'down', as you call it? This period of depression? Mightn't he have drowned himself then?"

"I don't know. I can only guess, though if my interpretation of his character's accurate he'd have been more likely to get stinking drunk, go to a brothel or find some tart."

Which is more or less what he did do, Tansey thought, remembering what Emma Watson had said about consoling Steve after Amanda Hulton had turned him down. "Nevertheless, he did take his own life, Mr White. There seems no doubt about that."

"None. He left a note, and there were no suspicious circumstances — at least none that surfaced at the inquest." Greg shook his head sadly. "I was away at the time, conducting a summer course in the States. It happened several weeks after the end of the Trinity term, you know. I was horrified, shocked, when I returned and learnt about it. I couldn't help reproaching myself. Who knows, if I'd been here . . . ? I always got on well with Steve."

"Is there any possibility that he took his life because he'd discovered that he'd got a worse degree than he'd hoped for? As far as he was concerned, this might have been the last straw, so to speak."

"But — Chief Inspector, you're misinformed on two counts. Steve was already dead when the results were announced. And he didn't get a poor degree. He didn't get a degree of any kind. He failed."

"Failed? Completely? That's unusual, surely?"

"Yes. I couldn't believe it. When we discussed his papers immediately after the exams he was pretty happy about how he'd done; he was possibly over-optimistic, I thought, but I never imagined he'd made such a mess of things. I even went to the Master to see if I could get his papers reviewed for the sake of Steve's family, but Sir Philip took a poor view. He said Steve had brought enough disgrace on St Xavier's by committing suicide because of a love-affair that he should have known was impossible, and it was best to forget the whole matter."

"Did you ever meet Steve's family?"

"Yes. I went to see them. I felt I should. They were a surprisingly elderly couple to have such a young son. He must have been an afterthought, and as so often happens in such cases he was their favourite."

"There were other sons?"

"Two, I believe, but — "

"Did you tell the Sarsons you'd tried to get Steve's papers re-assessed?"

"No. Definitely not. I told no one, and there was no one else present when I went to see the Master except the Senior Tutor, Dr Dawson."

"The Dr Dawson who died?"

"Yes. He agreed with Pinel about Steve, and that was the end of it. But, Chief Inspector — "

"You can guess what I'm thinking, Mr White. This is the best lead I've had so far. I admit the motive's weak, but supposing Steve had somehow learnt about his failure and told his family, and then decided he couldn't face the future without the Hulton girl and without a degree."

"I don't see how he could conceivably have known the results in advance."

"Maybe not, but it's a possibility to think about. Anyway, I'll have to look into the Sarsons. Meanwhile, Mr White, I hope you'll consider the conversation we've had this afternoon as strictly confidential."

"Of course, Chief Inspector, of course." Greg sighed. "And I hope to God you're right. When I think of Rosemary being hurt I desperately want an end to this business before — before anything else happens."

★ ★ ★

Sunday was another beautiful day. Greg, who was by nature a sedentary man, felt the urge to go for a long walk in the country, but he knew that this was impossible. Jean had been naturally upset when she had returned home the afternoon before to be confronted with what had happened to Rosemary. She

254

had blamed Tansey and the police, Greg and even Rosemary herself. The argument — still unresolved — about what Rosemary should do during the week to come had been bitter. No, thought Greg, a walk was out of the question; Jean would consider it to be a form of desertion. He retreated to his study, and sank into a chair.

He had been awake during much of the previous night, brooding over his talk with Tansey. He had assured the Chief Inspector that Steve Sarson couldn't have known about his exam results before he had decided to kill himself, but doubt about the validity of this assurance had begun to worry him. Could he have been wrong? Had Steve somehow learnt of his failure before the lists had been published?

Greg's original self-reproaches had returned to bother him again. He felt that as Steve's tutor he should have been insistent about inquiring fully into Steve's pathetic results. But he had been exhausted after a hectic time in the States, the boy was dead — making his lack of a degree irrelevant — and the Master, backed by the Senior Tutor, had been very firm on the subject. In retrospect he wondered why they had been so adamant; a few words in private with the Chairman of the Examining Board would surely not have revived the scandal of Steve's suicide. Of course the Master had claimed that he had already made inquiries and had been informed that Steve's papers had been abysmal.

But why had they been so abysmal? Steve certainly was not stupid. Admittedly he had been slack during his last year, but he had done enough work in the preceding two to enable him to get at worst a Third, and he said he had liked the papers. He had even remarked that he had been lucky in the topics he had chosen for his last minute revisions.

Sighing, Greg got to his feet. The door of the study was open, and he could hear sounds suggesting that Jean was getting tea. At least he could carry a tray up to Rosemary, who was spending the day in bed, and save Jean a journey. He was in the hall when the crash came. Jean ran out of the kitchen.

"What was that?"

"I don't know. It sounded like breaking glass. I think it came from the sitting-room."

Greg was right. There was a shattered pane in the middle of the window that faced the road, and shards of glass were scattered far into the room. The cause lay on the carpet, a reddish-brown object, rectangular in shape, about nine inches by four inches, with a large luggage label tied to it with a piece of string.

"Are you all right, sir?" The anxious face of the policeman on duty appeared outside the window. What with Rosemary being knocked down, his failure to get the number of the van, and now this, he was having a bad weekend. "I'm sorry. I tried to catch him but he was too quick for me."

"We're all right." Greg was studying the object on the floor. For a moment he had feared it might be a bomb, but now he saw that it was obviously a simple brick. He bent to pick it up.

"Don't touch it!" said the officer.

"But it's only a brick."

"Still, you never know, sir. May I come in?"

"Of course."

The officer spoke into his mobile phone as Greg, ignoring Jean's protest, went into the hall to open the front door for him.

"Was it the white van again, Constable?"

"No, sir. A chap on a motorbike, which took me by surprise. It was a mighty throw," he added, his voice tinged with admiration, as he inspected the object.

"And what do you mean by that?" Jean demanded. "He could have blown up the house while you were admiring his throwing arm. You call this protection?"

"Jean!" Greg protested.

"What does that label say?"

The officer had put on a glove and, without moving the brick, held up the label by its edges. They could all see that letters and whole words from a newspaper had been carefully pasted together so as to form a text. It read: "That was a warning. R, keep your mouth shut or next time it will be for real."

"It's meant for Rosemary, Jean. A threat."

"Obviously."

"Don't touch it or move it, please," repeated the officer. "They're sending a couple of men up to take it away."

"God! Not more police," said Jean.

The constable tactfully remarked that he would go and wait for his colleagues outside, and Jean turned on Greg.

"Now perhaps you'll listen to me," she said. "Those men told us they were satisfied with the results of their bomb, and that there'd be no more violence and no harm would come to us, *providing* we kept our mouths shut and played dumb. But did we? Were we sensible? No! You and Rosemary have both gone out of your way to help the police — especially Rosemary. I suppose she likes to feel important, but she was following your example. It's madness, I tell you! All that's happened is that the three of us are at risk. Greg, don't you realize that we're the only witnesses? Without us — "

Greg cut her short. "Which is all the more reason why we should do our best to put these men behind bars. We won't be really safe till they are. We had to go along with them in the beginning, allow ourselves to be blackmailed because the odds were so much against us. But the situation's changed, Jean. We're in a much stronger position. We've got to fight back."

"What for? Abstract justice? I've never heard such bloody nonsense. It's not as if you cared about old Pinel."

"Maybe not, but — " Greg thought of Ailsa Mackay and the Bursar and Tony Pulent and the Fremont brothers; he cared about all of them. "We'll talk about Rosemary later," he said forcefully. "I think maybe it would be best if she goes to stay with my parents for a while, even if it means missing some school. She can always have some extra coaching later."

"In that case," said Jean coldly, "I shall go and stay with my sister. I'm sure you'll be happy in your damned College, Greg."

★ ★ ★

But by Monday morning Rosemary was running a high temperature. The doctor diagnosed the virus that was prevalent

260

throughout the Thames Valley. He said it wasn't serious and she would be fine in a few days, but there was no question of her going to stay with her grandparents at present.

16

WHEN the Chief Inspector arrived at St Xavier's on Monday morning he found Greg White in the room which had become Ailsa Mackay's temporary office. He inquired after Rosemary, and was glad to hear that, as she seemed to have caught a virus, there had been no difficulty in persuading her to stay at home.

Pleasantries over, he said, "Miss Mackay, I wonder if you could give me any information about the Sarson family?"

"The Sarsons? Steve Sarson's family?" Ailsa couldn't resist glancing at Greg before she answered.

Tansey was amused. "Have you been doing my job for me, Mr White?"

"Not really. I'm trying to salve my conscience. Steve was my pupil and I'm certain he ought not to have failed his Finals. So at last I intend to look into the matter. Rather late in the day, I admit."

"Have you got anywhere?"

"I've confirmed that Steve drowned himself *before* the results of his Finals were made public. I've also looked up the name of the professor who chaired the examining board that failed Steve. I know him, though not well, and I thought I might go and have a word with him. Is that all right with you, Chief Inspector?"

"I don't see why not." Tansey was hesitant. "But don't mention any police interest in the Sarsons. Make some other excuse for your inquiry."

"Of course."

"Why *are* the police interested?" Ailsa inquired.

Again Tansey hesitated. Then, "In confidence, Miss Mackay, it's possible that the Sarsons might have considered they had a grudge against St Xavier's because of Steve's death."

"And so they decided to blow up the Master's Lodgings?" Ailsa was incredulous. She shook her head. "No, Chief Inspector. After Steve was drowned I went to see his parents in Colombury — that's in the Cotswolds not very far from here — "

"I know it," said Tansey.

"Well," went on Ailsa, "the family had been living there for some years. I know, because we've still got Steve's file and it shows that it was from a Colombury address that he applied for a place at St Xavier's. The family ran some sort of business there, I believe. Anyway, his mother and father were a pleasant old couple, dreadfully upset when I saw them, naturally. Steve had obviously been the apple of their eye and they were tremendously proud of him, but as far as I could make out there was no question of them blaming St Xavier's. On the contrary, they kept repeating how kind Greg had been to Steve, giving him free extra coaching and inviting him to his home and so forth."

Tansey refrained from remarking that Greg White as an individual was not quite identical with the College as an institution, and certainly not synonymous with its Master.

"Miss Mackay, you said they *were* a pleasant couple?" he remarked.

"I see what you mean. Yes, 'were' is right. Unfortunately Mrs Sarson died a few months after Steve. I'm not quite sure, but I think Mr Sarson stayed on in Colombury and a daughter or daughter-in-law keeps house for the family."

"I see," said Tansey. "About the family — Steve had brothers, didn't he?"

"Two." It was Greg who answered. "Older than he was, and apparently not academic material. I think they probably left school at sixteen. Steve was the clever one."

"His cleverness doesn't seem to have brought him good fortune," said Tansey, who himself had always regretted that his own education had been curtailed by his father's early death.

★ ★ ★

Half an hour later Chief Inspector Tansey was once more on his way to the Cotswolds, but this morning Sergeant Abbot was driving him. Bill Abbot had been born and brought up in Colombury and, though he no longer lived there, he knew the small market town well, had retained many contacts in the place and had often proved a useful source of information on the area.

"Sergeant, do you know a Colombury family by the name of Sarson?"

"Sarson? That's the name of the boy that drowned himself, sir." Abbot took his eyes off the road and looked at his superior inquiringly.

"Yes," replied the Chief Inspector, without further comment.

Abbot knew better than to ask further questions. Instead, he said, "There's a furniture business called that in Colombury, sir, but it's not been there long, about five years, I think. I don't know the people who run it."

"What sort of furniture business?"

"Nothing superior, sir. Not a real antique business or anything like that. I believe they buy second-hand stuff, do it up and sell it. There's a fair demand, and I'd imagine they make a reasonable living. But Sergeant Court will be our man. He's the authority on newish people in Colombury."

"Yes, I suppose so. Anyway, we'll have to make our mark at the police station before we do anything else."

Tansey hoped he didn't sound too

reluctant. Sergeant Court was indeed an authority on Colombury and its inhabitants, and protocol demanded that they should call on him if they were to operate on his patch. But Court, now on the point of retiring, had always been a slow-speaking, slow-moving, slow-thinking officer who loved a good gossip, and Tansey visualized hours wasting away over cups of sugary tea.

He was not far wrong. By the time they left the Colombury police station he and Abbot were ready for a pint of beer and a good meal — both of which were readily obtained at the Windrush Arms. Nevertheless, the conversation with Sergeant Court had not been a waste of time. They had learnt quite a lot about the Sarsons.

Abbot had been correct when he said that the Sarsons had come to Colombury five years ago, and Court had been able to add that they had moved from Reading. They had bought a derelict house on the outskirts of the town with a variety of outbuildings, and had set up their business there. At that time the family had consisted of the elderly couple, Mr and Mrs Roger Sarson, and their son Bert and his wife Meg, who had two children. Bert's two brothers, Tom and young Steve lived at home and completed the group. They appeared to be an exceptionally close family, but they were not disliked in the town. They worked hard and had made a comparative success of their enterprise. They had never given the police any trouble — there had never been any suspicion of dealing in stolen goods, for example — though among the girls in the district Tom had a good or bad reputation, depending on the individual concerned.

The family had been devastated by Steve's death. Mrs Sarson had died shortly afterwards, and her death was said to be a direct result of the loss of her favourite son. As far as Sergeant Court knew, there had not been the slightest suggestion that the Sarsons blamed the University or St Xavier's College for Steve's suicide. The reasons generally accepted for the tragedy had been overwork and an unhappy love-affair.

"Not very encouraging," Tansey said

as he and Abbot finished their meal. "These Sarsons sound an exemplary bunch — except perhaps for Tom. But his name, common as it may be, is another coincidence. I think we'd better go and have a look at them, Sergeant."

★ ★ ★

Following Sergeant Court's instructions, Abbot had no difficulty in locating the Sarsons' establishment. It was not impressive, merely a collection of untidy buildings on an uncared-for area of land. One building bore a dilapidated sign: 'Sarson & Sons, Reconditioned Furniture'. As Abbot drew up, two toddlers, playing with a ball on a scrubby piece of grass in front of the ugly red-brick house, stopped their game to stare, and a mongrel dog, chained to its makeshift kennel, began to bark furiously.

The police officers had scarcely got out of their car when a woman appeared at the front door of the house. She was about thirty, and thin to the point of scrawniness. As if for protection, the toddlers at once ran to her and clung to her apron.

"Yes?" she said, pleasantly enough. "What can I do for you? I'm afraid my husband's out, but if there's anything you were particularly looking for, I'm sure I could — "

"We're police officers," interrupted Tansey. "Detective Chief Inspector Tansey and Detective-Sergeant Abbot from the Thames Valley Police," he announced, holding out his warrant card.

The woman's manner changed perceptibly. "And just what do you want?" she demanded aggressively. "We've never had no trouble here."

"What we want is to speak to Mr Sarson?"

"Which one? I told you my husband was out."

"Mr Roger Sarson — Mr Sarson senior."

"Why?"

"We'll tell him that when we see him."

"He's an old man and none too well. He had a stroke a few months ago. I'm his daughter-in-law, Meg Sarson."

"Mrs Sarson, we still need to speak to your father-in-law. I'm sorry about his health, but we'll be as considerate as we can."

Meg Sarson gave a shrug of disgusted resignation. "Oke!" she said.

She turned away before she saw the expression on Tansey's face as she used the slightly unusual — almost old-fashioned — slang. Shooshing the children back outside, she led the two men into the house and showed them into a front room. It was neat and clean, but gave the impression of being little used.

"Sit down," she said, somewhat more amiably. "I'll fetch him."

Tansey sat, but Abbot strolled across to the fireplace and studied the photographs on the mantel. He had been attracted to them because they seemed to be mostly of the Sarson children at various ages, and he liked children. But, close to them, his attention was immediately seized by a coloured print of a bride and her groom. The bride was a younger, plumper version of the woman who had let them into the house; the groom, several inches shorter — a square-set, sandy-haired man — was presumably Bert Sarson, and he was in an army sergeant's uniform. Abbot stared at the photograph, then suddenly stiffened.

"Sir, you'd better have a look at this," he said hurriedly as there were sounds in the passage outside the door.

Tansey had just time to take a quick glance at the wedding photograph and resume his seat before Meg Sarson brought in her father-in-law. Like his eldest son, he was a short, thick-set man. His greying hair showed signs of having once been sandy, and his eyes were a watery blue. He moved slowly, dragging his carpet-slippered feet across the floor, until he sank into an upright chair. Probably he was only in his mid-sixties, but it was difficult to visualize him as the father of Steve who, had he lived, would have been twenty-two or twenty-three by now.

"We're sorry to bother you, Mr Sarson, but we wonder if you'd mind answering a few questions," Tansey said.

"Same if I do," said Sarson, clearly a man of few words.

"You've heard about the explosion at St Xavier's College in Oxford," Tansey began.

"Saw about it on the telly."

"Your son, Steve, was a student there. You must have been proud of him." Tansey paused as Sarson grunted his assent. "And his death must have been a great shock." Sarson grunted again. "Did he enjoy being at the College?" This time Sarson nodded without speaking. "What did he think of Mr White, his tutor?"

At last there was a positive response. "Steve liked Mr White and his family very much. Mr White's a good man, and he was kind to Steve. We're glad he wasn't hurt by that bomb."

"But his daughter's been hurt, deliberately knocked off her bike."

Involuntarily Sarson looked at his daughter-in-law, as if for confirmation. "I — I didn't know," he said. "Why? I don't understand." He sounded miserable and upset.

"How could you know, Pa?" Meg Sarson was quick to intervene. "There's been nothing on the telly or in the papers, has there?" She addressed Tansey. "How was the girl knocked down?"

"By a white van."

"Really. There's lots of those about. We've got one ourselves, to move light furniture around."

Tansey didn't bother to ask where the van had been on Saturday afternoon. He spoke directly to the old man. "To return to Steve, Mr Sarson, were you annoyed when, after all the sacrifices you and your family had made, he didn't manage to get a degree?"

When Sarson didn't answer at once Tansey thought he hadn't heard the question. Then Sarson burst out. "It was a lie! A lie! Steve was a clever boy. He didn't — "

"Pa!" In three strides Meg Sarson had crossed the room and was standing over her father-in-law, shielding him from Tansey's sight. She muttered something inaudible, and the old man started to whimper. She turned on the Chief Inspector. "See what you've done. You've upset him. I told you he wasn't well. Half the time he doesn't know what he's doing or saying. You'd better clear out, the two of you!"

"Yes, of course, Mrs Sarson." Tansey made no attempt to argue with her. Signalling to Abbot, he rose to his feet. "Goodbye, and thank you for your help."

"What help?" she demanded, but received no answer.

As Tansey and Abbot came out of the house the dog started barking again, but the children had disappeared. Their voices could be heard calling to each other from one of the outhouses. Then a white van, a table tied to its roof, trundled up the lane and parked beside the unmarked police car. Two men emerged; they were both sandy-haired, blue-eyed and red-faced. The taller and younger man had a crooked nose, which looked as if it might have been broken in a fight.

"Good morning, sirs," the older of the pair greeted them politely. "How can we be of help? We've some nice stuff at the moment. Sorry we weren't here when you arrived, but we've been to a sale in Chipping Norton. Incidentally, I'm Bert Sarson. My brother, Tom." He gestured.

"Police officers, not customers," Tansey said, announcing their names and ranks.

"My warrant card." He held it out, but Bert waved it away.

"What's the trouble? Stolen goods? We never deal in them, Chief Inspector."

"Nothing like that, Mr Sarson. We came to see your father."

"Pa?" Did the laugh that followed ring hollow? "What on earth would you want with Pa? He hardly leaves the house, and I doubt if he's got the brains to mastermind a crime any more — if he ever did."

"Nevertheless, he was most helpful."

"You've seen him?" Bert sounded wary.

"What was he helpful about?" It was Tom who couldn't resist the question.

"About your brother Steve."

"He's dead!"

"Yes, indeed. I commiserate." Tansey opened the car door and started to get in, then seemed to have second thoughts. "By the way, Mr Sarson, when did you leave the army?"

"Five years ago, Chief Inspector. I'd done my time and I decided not to sign on again." Bert Sarson spoke casually, but to Tansey he appeared to have tensed. "I was married and my wife was expecting our second baby. It seemed sensible to settle down in business with my father."

"Very sensible," said Tansey, turning to the car. Then once more he changed his mind. "May we have a look at your stock now we're here? You never know — "

There was only a slight hesitation before Bert answered, "Of course." He led the way to the largest of the outbuildings, while Tansey and Abbot glanced around curiously. "This is the showroom," Bert added a trifle pompously. The workshops are over there." He pointed to a couple of rusty Nissen huts.

Tansey seemed satisfied with only a cursory inspection of the varied collection of bits of furniture and other bric-à-brac that Sarson & Sons were offering for sale. Then he said, "Well, many thanks. We must be off. Goodbye to you."

As they drove away Abbot said, "You saw what I saw in that photograph, sir? It was a clear print, and the regimental badges were unmistakable. Bert Sarson was a sapper — a Royal Engineer."

"I saw," replied Tansey. "And did you notice the motorbike between a couple of those derelict buildings?"

"Indeed, sir," said Abbot.

Tansey relapsed into silence. He was glad he couldn't read the Sarson family's thoughts. He guessed that one or two of them at least were wishing him every ill. Nevertheless, he was elated. He was sure in his own mind that he had traced the villains. The next step was to prove it — and he guessed that would be far from simple.

17

"**Y**OU'VE put up a reasonable case, Chief Inspector."

He didn't add, "But not good enough." It wasn't necessary. Tansey knew the Chief Constable's habits. He would now delve and probe and, unless Tansey could produce convincing arguments to support his hypotheses, his so-called case would be shredded.

"You're happy about it, in your own mind?" Midvale inquired, shifting his bulk in the large chair that had been specially made for him. "No doubts? No doubts at all? But of course you've got doubts."

"Of course, sir." Tansey found he had no alternative but to acquiesce.

The Chief Inspector glanced around the Chief Constable's office, hoping to gain inspiration from somewhere or something — the Bratby hanging on the wall behind Midvale's desk, for example, or even the plain Wilton carpet on the floor. The more he had considered Bert and Tom Sarson, the more convinced he had become that they were guilty of the bomb outrage at St Xavier's; but he was fully aware that the evidence he had so far obtained against them was circumstantial, and their apparent motive terribly weak. In other circumstances he would have been content to wait, to dig deeper, to repeat interviews, to follow up seemingly useless leads. But now he was fearful, pressured by a need for urgency.

He was fearful for the Whites, and for Rosemary in particular. She was the only witness who might be able to identify Tom — and Tom probably knew it. What was more, Tom, unlike his brother Bert, appeared to be an impulsive character, lacking in common sense. It had been foolish in the extreme to attempt to rape Rosemary after her abortive effort to escape through the bathroom window, when his brother was waiting downstairs and highly unlikely to countenance such a crime. And, in fact, if he had not made this stupid attempt, Rosemary would never have seen his face.

It had been equally foolish to knock

her off her bicycle especially with a van that could have been identified — and equally foolish to threaten her. This last effort had merely tended to confirm that she could have and indeed had recognized him. And it followed that, once Tom felt that the police were moving in on him, he would try some other violent means to silence Rosemary.

"Let's consider just what you've got on this family," said the Chief Constable. As he spoke he ticked off the points one by one on his broad fingers. "Fact one: the brothers are the right height and build to fit the villains as described by all the Whites, and one is called Tom. Two: the Sarson family have a connection with St Xavier's through Steve. Three: because of Steve they knew of Mr White and liked him, and the senior villain emphasized throughout the episode that they intended no harm should come to the Whites. Four: Bert was a sapper, and it's possible he could have had a knowledge of explosives — incidentally, have we been on to the Met to ask the Ministry of Defence about the details of his record?"

"Yes, sir, but it's taking time."

"Well, let's go on. Fact five: The Sarsons run a white van and a motorcycle. Six: they seem to favour the word 'oke' rather than the more usual 'OK'. And seven: Rosemary White believes she can identify Tom."

Midvale sighed. "As I said, Chief Inspector, taken together the points I've enumerated add up to quite a good case, but all the same I can't see the DPP buying it. Quite apart from a competent barrister, any third-year law student would take it fact by fact, and treat them individually with derision. The DPP would argue that any cumulative effect would be lost in the confusion of a trial. In fact, what you've done is prove that the Sarsons — together with a few other people — *might well* have committed the crime. Even Rosemary White's identification isn't worth much. The girl admits she only caught a glimpse of the villain's face, and any defence counsel would make a lot of the point that she was under considerable stress at the time. Then he would argue that Rosemary White saw Tom Sarson in the street and, because of a chance resemblance, she imagined that he and her assailant were one and the same. An identity parade would be useless. You follow my train of thought, Chief Inspector? You agree?"

"Yes, sir," said Tansey. There was nothing else he could say.

"And as yet we haven't come to the major weakness in the case against the Sarsons — the fact that they have no clear motive. Steve had already taken his exams and gone down from the University when he drowned himself. The family had no reason to connect his death with St Xavier's, especially as, according to the evidence at the inquest, he had taken his life because at the time he was depressed over a love-affair that had turned out badly."

"Are you suggesting I should forget the Sarsons, sir?" Tansey was becoming slightly annoyed at this shredding of his case.

"No! Don't be silly, Dick. I'm merely suggesting that you should keep an open mind." Unexpectedly the Chief Constable gave Tansey a broad smile. "And I also suggest that you review the case from the beginning. You may well be right about the Sarsons, but you need to plug the holes."

★ ★ ★

Dick Tansey sat in his office, thinking of holes and manholes and manhole covers. The Chief Constable had done his best to fragment his case, but he still believed in it. Admittedly, some of the evidence he had collected could be applied against persons (so far unknown) other than the Sarsons — but only when taken item by item. Nevertheless, there were two holes that were really worrying: the lack of motive, a most annoying point that he had appreciated all along; and Rosemary's identification, about which he had previously felt reasonably secure.

He decided to tackle the second, and simpler, part of the evidence first. Obeying the Chief Constable's injunctions, he re-read the files that related to Rosemary's description of the man who had attempted to rape her — or whom she thought was about to attempt to rape her. He had always been impressed by the common sense that the girl had shown, and the lack of diffidence with which she had treated the matter. He was pleased to note now that from the beginning, before she had helped the artist create an impression of Tom, and before she had seen Tom in the street, she had mentioned his crooked nose. This was not a characteristic that she was likely to have invented and, he was sure, it went a long way towards validating Rosemary's identification. That hole could fairly be said to have been plugged.

The lack of motive presented far more of a problem. If the Sarsons were the villains, the motive had to be connected with Steve, and the Master had to have been the prime, though perhaps not the sole, target of the bomb attack, for no one could have known in advance precisely which of the senior dons — apart from Pinel himself — might or might not be present at a particular meeting in the Lodgings. It followed then that the Sarsons — if they were guilty — believed, rightly or wrongly, that

Sir Philip Pinel had done Steve some immeasurable harm — a harm that had to be avenged.

But what harm or injury would warrant such a violent attack on the Master, his senior staff and the College, Tansey failed to imagine. Nor were the files any help. In spite of his sense of urgency, he realized that he would have to start again, interviewing the same individuals, but possibly asking different questions. He needed to know a great deal more about Steve Sarson than had so far been unearthed.

Since he felt that it was vital not to arouse any suspicions in the minds of the Sarsons that the police had more than a passing interest in them, Tansey decided to ignore them for the moment and to commence his new round of inquiries with Greg White. From what he already knew of Steve, the young man's behaviour seemed to have been reasonably understandable, except in one respect — his failure to get any sort of degree. Clearly this fact had puzzled White, who had been his tutor, and old Mr Sarson's reaction to a query about his son's misfortune had been, to say the least, peculiar.

Was there any way in which the results of Steve's examinations could have been wrong or misinterpreted? Tansey put the question to Greg, whom he found the next morning in his rooms in the College, in conversation with Ailsa Mackay. Neither could produce an adequate answer.

At last Ailsa said, "Isn't it possible that old Mr Sarson refuses to believe that his clever son could have failed?"

"Sure," Tansey agreed, but he remembered how quick Meg Sarson had been to interrupt her father-in-law, and to emphasize that he was not altogether a 'responsible' witness.

He said, "Mr White, you told me you were going to contact the head of the examining board about Steve Sarson."

"Yes. I've done that, Chief Inspector, and I've also talked again to Dr Cathcart. At present Cathcart's at home recovering from peritonitis, but normally he's in charge of the language side of St Xavier's English teaching. He repeated what he'd told me before. He had been surprised that Steve hadn't got a degree, and when he asked about Steve's language papers he had been informed that they had been perfectly adequate. He had left it at that. It seems that it was the papers on English literature — my responsibility, Chief Inspector, and Steve's strong side — that had let him down. Professor Massey-King, the examiner, confirmed that."

"Something odd must have happened. You mustn't blame yourself, Greg," Ailsa said as he shook his head in disgust. "Perhaps Steve didn't feel well when he sat the papers, or he misread the questions or — "

"Nonsense!" Greg said savagely.

Ailsa shrugged; she knew his anger was not directed at her, and she insisted, "There must be some explanation, Greg."

"What I don't understand is why Steve should tell me that he'd liked the papers, that he'd been lucky in what he'd chosen for last-minute revision work and was sure he'd done well. It makes no sense. Why should he lie to me?" Greg demanded. "He must have known he'd made a mess of his chances."

"What exactly did Professor Massey-King say?" Tansey asked, trying to deflect Greg White from his futile recriminations.

"He wasn't very forthcoming." Greg gave a somewhat bitter laugh. "In fact, he was damned unhelpful. All he'd say was that what Steve had offered in the way of literature papers had made it impossible to award him a degree of any kind."

"Is Massey-King always so uncooperative?" Tansey inquired.

"I don't know him well, but I wouldn't have thought so." Greg was doubtful. "Perhaps he'd had a bad egg for breakfast when I saw him. Anyway, he flatly refused to discuss the subject further. He said it was past history, and it would be a mistake to rake over the dirt now. Steve was dead. It was a great pity, but nothing could be done about it."

"How unkind!" said Ailsa. "He sounds appalling."

Tansey hesitated. "Mr White, Professor Massey-King used the word dirt?"

"Yes. I must admit I thought it a bit odd."

"Well, this may sound an odd question,

but did it strike you that Massey-King was at all nervous or personally upset that you'd re-opened this matter?"

"I'm not sure what you're getting at, Chief Inspector." Greg looked questioningly at Tansey. "Professor Massey-King is not a nervous type, but in retrospect I suppose I did have an impression that he was irritated — or perhaps embarrassed — but I could easily be wrong."

"I see. Many thanks, Mr White," said Tansey, and thought that it might be a good idea if he himself were to pay a call on this Professor Massey-King.

★ ★ ★

Professor Massey-King was a tall and handsome man, with grey hair and a florid complexion. He had an autocratic air and, as soon as his secretary had shown Tansey into his study, distanced himself from the Chief Inspector by waving him to a chair without speaking. He did not rise from behind his desk, nor did he offer his hand. Instead, he continued to glance through some documents for a moment or two, remaining perfectly polite but implying that he was in a commanding position and that his time was valuable.

"What is this about, Chief Inspector? My secretary says you refused to tell her. It sounds unduly enigmatic."

"Not really, sir, but it *is* confidential, which is one of the reasons I have come without my sergeant. I'm making inquiries about a member of the University who drowned himself last year. His name was Steve Sarson."

"Steve Sarson? Why come to me? He wasn't at this College and I never taught him."

Professor Massey-King spoke in a mildly bored tone and his expression remained calm, but Tansey was watching his hands which, fingertips together, had been forming a casual pyramid on his desktop. Tansey was sure he saw the fingers tense, then relax, and he knew that this Professor was not at ease.

"But I'm told you were responsible for his failure to get a degree, sir."

"Not I, Chief Inspector. Sarson was responsible for that himself."

"I'm sorry. I see your point. I worded my sentence badly. But perhaps you'd be good enough to explain exactly what *you* mean, sir. I gather he was a clever young man."

"That's as may be. All I know is that the English literature papers he offered were not adequate for him to be awarded a degree." Massey-King paused; if he had briefly felt insecure, the moment had passed. "Chief Inspector, I don't imagine you understand how the system functions, but there could have been nothing personal about the examiners' decision to fail Sarson. Papers are anonymous when they are marked and classified."

Tansey, feeling frustrated, tried another tack. "Could Sarson have known about his failure before the results were published? Could this have been a contributory cause for his suicide?"

"It's — possible, Chief Inspector."

Tansey noticed the hesitation. He saw Massey-King stare at him, and sensed that the Professor would very much prefer to bring the interview to a close. Though Massey-King had appeared to be completely frank, he had shown a certain tension that one wouldn't have expected if he had been indifferent to, or objective about, the subject under discussion.

"I must ask you a direct question, sir," Tansey said quickly. "To the best of your knowledge, did Steve Sarson know about his failure to get a degree before he committed suicide?"

Massey-King took his time before answering. At last he said, "Chief Inspector, I don't think I'm prepared to answer your question unless you can give me a good reason for it."

"That's simple, sir." Tansey was blunt. "The Master's Lodgings at St Xavier's College have been partially destroyed by a bomb. People have been injured. The Senior Tutor has since died — "

"I know! I know all that." Massey-King interrupted. His air of superiority had deserted him, and he was clearly shaken. "But what's that to do with Steve Sarson? It's over a year since the suicide and the boy's dead. It never occurred to me that there could be any connection with the St Xavier's bombing."

"To be honest, sir, I'm not certain there

is a connection, but there's circumstantial evidence pointing in that direction, and I need to know if the Sarsons had any reason to harbour a grudge against the Master and St Xavier's."

"I see. The simple answer to that is no!"

"I have to judge that for myself, sir."

Massey-King gave Tansey a calculating stare. "Very well, Chief Inspector," he said reluctantly, "I'll tell you what happened, as simply as I can."

Steve Sarson had sat his Finals and his papers had been duly marked. Except for three of the English literature papers, he would have got a Second Class degree. These three papers were brilliant, and would have assured him a First. But — and this was a big but — they were too brilliant. A careful study of them revealed that Sarson had possibly seen the questions in advance and been able to prepare for them.

"You mean he'd cheated?"

Tansey was amazed. He remembered old Mr Sarson's words. "They lied," he'd said, "Steve was a clever boy. He didn't — " Then his daughter-in-law had shut him up. Didn't what? Didn't cheat — or perhaps didn't need to cheat?

"If you want to put it like that, yes, he cheated!" said Massey-King.

"How is it that this didn't become public knowledge?" Tansey asked suspiciously. "I'm surprised it wasn't a scandal at the time. Surely the media would have made a splash with it — especially after Sarson's suicide. Yet not even Mr White, Steve's tutor, knew about it."

Massey-King nodded slowly. "The whole affair was hushed up. With hindsight this may have been a mistake, but at the time . . . Chief Inspector, Sir Philip Pinel, the Master of St Xavier's, is a friend of mine. We were at school together and our families are close. When I suspected that Steve Sarson had cheated I went to see Philip Pinel. Naturally he was extremely upset. He had always had a very high regard for the reputation of his College, maintaining that one couldn't expect support for an institution with poor standards of conduct. Pinel was afraid that the College would hardly survive such a scandal.

"Anyway Pinel sent for Steve and

confronted him with the evidence for our suspicions. The Senior Tutor was also present, I believe. At first Sarson denied the accusation vehemently, but then he admitted it and agreed to have the papers in question withdrawn. Twenty-four hours later his body was pulled out of the Cherwell."

"Poor young man."

"Yes. It was sad, Chief Inspector, I agree. It also left us with a problem. In the circumstances he couldn't be awarded a degree, even posthumously, as it were. That would have been highly immoral. On the other hand he was dead, and there was no point in a scandal that would harm his memory and his family — "

"And St Xavier's College?"

"That too!" Massey-King gave a thin smile. "So the papers in question were destroyed and his name was omitted from the published class lists. I had some words with the examiners who had seen them, and scarcely anyone else inquired about the case. If they did, it wasn't difficult to dissemble."

"His family?"

"Not as far as I know. I imagine they were too concerned over his death to worry about exam results, and the Master would have dealt with any questions they might have had easily enough. It was made plain at the inquest that Steve took his life because of an affair with a girl that turned out badly. This could also have affected how he coped with his examination and explained why he failed to get a degree."

"Yes indeed," Tansey said absently. He was thinking that yet again a scandal threatening St Xavier's and its Master had been conveniently avoided.

18

"I DO not believe it, Chief Inspector." Greg White emphasized each word separately. "I know you've told us that Massey-King says that Steve admitted it to the Master, but in spite of that I'd as soon believe that Tony Pulent — whom I've known all his life — was a cheat. I grant that Steve Sarson was an odd mixture. He was to some extent street-wise, as they say, but he was also disingenuous. Above all, he was proud, proud of what he'd already accomplished, and of what he hoped to achieve in the future. He would *not* have stooped to cheating."

"Not even if he'd been afraid of getting a poor degree?" Tansey asked tentatively. "You said yourself that he hadn't done much work in his last year."

"He already had a good job lined up, hadn't he?" Peter Lacque remarked before White could answer.

The three men were in the Bursar's

office where Tansey had tracked down Greg White. The Chief Inspector had told them in confidence what he had learnt from Professor Massey-King. He was intrigued by their reactions.

"Yes. He'd been offered a lectureship at London University." White replied to the Bursar's question, and added for Tansey's benefit, "Not terribly well-paid but a fine beginning for an academic career. London would naturally have been disappointed if Steve hadn't got his First — and so would he, though he'd not really done enough work recently to deserve it, as you suggested, Chief Inspector. Nevertheless, I doubt if they'd have reneged on their offer, not unless his results had been very poor."

"All right," said Tansey. "I accept your opinion, as far as it goes. Steve Sarson was an unlikely character to cheat, and there was no great pressing reason for him to do so. But still, what about opportunity?"

"That's something I fail to understand," said Lacque. "How could he have seen the papers in advance? They're always most jealously guarded."

"Have there been similar cases before — proved cases, I mean? Have papers ever been sold, for instance?"

"Not to my knowledge, though I suppose it could have happened in the past, when security might have been more lax."

"Anyway, I'm sure Steve wouldn't have had the money to buy them — or know how to set about it," White objected.

"Then what would you say to accident?" asked Tansey. "Accidents do happen. The most responsible people seem to leave briefcases full of vital documents in taxis or trains. Couldn't a forgetful professor have left the exam questions out on his desk, and mightn't Steve have been tempted?"

"What forgetful professor, and where?"

"You tell me, Mr White!" Tansey had momentarily lost patience with the conversation, which was getting him nowhere. "Let's face the fact of Steve's admission. I reiterate that Massey-King claims that Steve Sarson admitted to your Master, Sir Philip Pinel, that he'd cheated. Now you're trying to persuade me that Steve couldn't possibly have done so. Can you explain that anomaly?"

"No, I can't, Chief Inspector. You'll have to ask the Master. Let's hope he can explain, though I have my doubts. All I know is that no one at St Xavier's can have had any advance knowledge of or connection with the examination papers for the English School. So how and where could Steve have seen them?" White turned to the Bursar. "You agree, Philip?"

"Yes, Greg, I — I agree."

But Tansey noticed the slight hesitation in the Bursar's reply. He watched as Peter Lacque picked up a pen from his desk and played with it, before seeming to come to a decision.

"I do have a thought about a possible connection," he said. "I'm afraid it's pretty far-fetched, but — "

"That doesn't matter," Tansey said quickly. "The oddest scrap of information sometimes helps."

Lacque still seemed reluctant to speak, but eventually he said, "It's about Emma Watson, who was on the staff here until recently." He spent a couple of minutes repeating what both his listeners knew

301

before he came to his point. "I remember that in the Trinity Term before last she did some work for Professor Massey-King. His secretary was ill, and this was a particularly busy time for him. I'd heard he was in need of assistance, and I was aware that Emma could well do with some extra money, so I — I suggested she should help him out."

"You mean there's a possibility she might have seen the English Literature question papers?" Tansey said bluntly.

"Yes, a vague possibility," Lacque admitted, "but even if she had why should she have told Sarson about them?"

"He wasn't one of her pupils," said White. "She taught history, and I doubt that if she'd met Steve in the quad she could have put a name to him."

"Well, thanks all the same. I value your opinions." Tansey thoughtfully looked at his watch. He had decided to keep his own counsel about Emma Watson's relationship with Steve Sarson. "Quite clearly, I must make an effort to see Sir Philip."

★ ★ ★

302

The Chief Inspector's interview with the Master of St Xavier's was brief and largely pointless. Pinel made no pretence that the revival of the story of Steve Sarson's death and its probable causes had taken him by surprise. He was the first to introduce the subject.

"I've been talking to Professor Massey-King," he said, "and he tells me you're interested in Sarson's failure to get a degree, Chief Inspector. I follow your train of thought. You believe the Sarson family may have blamed me and the College for this misfortune, and decided to take matters into their own hands and exact some kind of revenge."

"Yes, sir," said Tansey. He couldn't refrain from adding, "You've put the case very clearly."

"Then I'll put this clearly too, Chief Inspector. That theory is all hogwash. Steve Sarson cheated over his examinations. He admitted it to me, and to save a lot of adverse publicity it was agreed that he would withdraw the papers in question — which meant that he hadn't offered sufficient to warrant a degree. He had reason to be grateful to me, not the reverse. It could have been very unpleasant for him if I hadn't offered him this way out, but had taken further action."

And it would have been unpleasant for the College too, Tansey thought. Aloud he said, "Did the family ever ask you about Steve's failure, sir?"

"No. I believe Miss Mackay, my secretary, went to see Sarson's parents, and I know that Mr White visited them later, after he came back from the United States. Of course, neither of them knew anything about the cheating."

"Did Steve Sarson explain to you how he managed to cheat?"

"I don't quite understand."

"Did he say where and when and how he learnt the details of the examination questions?"

"No."

"And you didn't inquire?"

"No," Sir Philip said shortly. "Chief Inspector, surely this is all irrelevant. If the Sarsons harboured any malice against me and St Xavier's over Steve's death, why didn't they take action months ago instead of waiting for more than a year?"

As he took his leave of the Master, Tansey had to admit that this was a valid point. Information he had received from the Ministry of Defence via the Met made it clear that Bert Sarson, as a result of his training and experience in the army, had the ability to make a simple explosive mixture and construct an explosive device whenever he wished. So why this long delay? Tansey could think of no answer to this poser.

* * *

The Chief Inspector's next move was to phone Emma Watson and ask her to meet him. She had been fetched out of a class and was not in the best of tempers. She said she was busy during the rest of the day, but when Tansey insisted agreed to meet him at the Saracen's Head in Abingdon at six o'clock that evening.

She arrived at six-thirty. Tansey was conscious of the admiring glances she received from the men leaning against the bar as she came across to the corner table he had secured. She didn't apologize for her unpunctuality. She sat down, unbuttoned her jacket to reveal a low-cut blouse and gave him a provocative smile.

"What, no sergeant, Mr Tansey? You're brave to come alone. What about your reputation?"

Tansey ignored the taunts. He summoned a waiter and ordered drinks. He had already decided how to deal with Miss Watson. In silence he waited for the return of the waiter.

Then he said suddenly, "Why did you lie to me the last time we met?"

"Lie to you?" Emma opened her eyes wide.

"You told me you'd had what you described as a 'one-night stand' with Steve Sarson. You knew him much better than that, didn't you?"

"What if I did, Chief Inspector? My sex life and his are no concern of yours. Especially now the poor boy's dead — "

"Because of you!"

"Me? Don't be a fool, Tansey. Steve would never have drowned himself for love of *me*. It was that Amanda Hulton he wanted, but I thought he'd more or less got over her. He told me he'd accepted that she wasn't for him. That's why his death was such a shock. I was really upset when I heard. I liked the boy. He didn't treat me like a tart as — as classy guys like Hugh Fremont did. He was a — a genuine person."

Tansey stared at her. He had to believe what she said. It would have taken a fine actress to put on such a performance without warning. Emma Watson had cared for Steve Sarson. She had done her best to comfort him. She'd assumed he'd taken his own life because of his unrequited love for Amanda Hulton. She obviously knew nothing about the accusation of cheating.

"I'm sorry," he said, though he wasn't sure why he was apologizing. He hurried on. "Miss Watson, I have other questions to ask you. During the Trinity Term of last year you did some work for Professor Massey-King. Is that correct?"

"Yes. That's right, but — "

"You knew he was the Chairman of the Examining Board for students taking their English Finals?"

Emma Watson nodded. "Of course. I did a lot of work for him while his regular secretary was away."

"And some of that was confidential work, Miss Watson. It would have been a great breach of confidentiality if you had betrayed any details of the examination papers to anyone — and particularly to anyone who was going to sit the examinations, wouldn't it? In fact, it would allow such an individual to cheat."

"Yes, I suppose — " Emma stopped abruptly. "Ye gods!" she exclaimed. "You're talking about Steve. But it wasn't like that. At least it wasn't meant to be. Steve would never have cheated, not knowingly."

She gulped down the remains of her gin and tonic and held out her empty glass; she had become quite pale. Tansey waved to the waiter and ordered another drink for her. He had scarcely touched his own whisky. He looked at Emma anxiously. She was clearly upset, but by the time the fresh drink had arrived she had largely regained her composure.

"Tell me what happened," Tansey said gently. "How could someone cheat unknowingly?"

"Well, one night Steve was explaining

that it was impossible to revise everything, and how there was a lot of luck in what one chose to do with limited time — which is true enough. And — and I don't know what got into me, except that I felt sorry for him. Anyway, I said, 'I'll make five choices for you,' and I did. Later he told me that three of them had proved to be right. I'd known they would be, because I'd seen the papers. Massey-King sometimes left various drafts on his desk."

"Didn't Steve suspect?"

"No. Why should he? He didn't know Massey-King was to be the chief examiner. He thought my choices were pure chance. Anyway, he could easily have decided to revise those particular subjects himself. And I didn't enlighten him. Term ended and I had other things on my mind."

"I'm afraid what you did was *not* trivial, Miss Watson. It was very important. Steve was accused of cheating, and as a result failed to get any kind of degree."

Emma was aghast. "And that's — that's why he committed suicide? You mean it was my fault? Oh shit! Why didn't he explain? I'd have supported him. Not that it would have helped him — not if that bastard Philip Pinel had anything to do with it." She paused, then ended miserably, "Oh poor, poor Steve! He was a clever boy. He didn't need to cheat."

"It's a sad story," Tansey agreed, "and it's not finished yet."

"What do you mean?" Emma was still thinking of Steve.

"Miss Watson, I'm telling you this in confidence. If any persons considered they had cause to bear a grudge against St Xavier's and its Master, surely they would be the Sarson family. And there are other reasons for suspecting that Steve's brothers, Bert and Tom, may have been responsible for the recent bomb outrage."

"Is that why you've been asking me all these questions?" Emma stared at him in horror. "Of course," she answered for herself. "How stupid of me. I should have realized but — but it was so long ago. Why should they have waited till now?"

It was the same weakness in the case against the Sarsons that Sir Philip

Pinel had spotted immediately. But, having found an excellent motive, Tansey was sure there would be a reasonable explanation — if only he could light upon it. He decided to pull in Bert and Tom for questioning the next day.

But a great deal was to happen before then.

* * *

Even in retrospect no one could blame the Chief Inspector's decision to wait until the next day before taking further action, or for the consequences of his decision. Where Tansey could be faulted was in his judgement of Emma Watson. He was right in his assessment that she had been appalled when she learnt that what had been intended as a friendly gesture towards a young man she liked had had such disastrous results. What he failed to appreciate was the extent of Emma's hatred for the Master of St Xavier's.

At eight o'clock that evening, as Dick Tansey and his wife Hilary were sitting down to supper, the telephone rang in the Sarsons' house on the outskirts of Colombury. Bert and Meg were upstairs putting their children to bed. The old man was asleep in front of the kitchen fire. Tom answered the phone.

When Tansey learnt of this much later he was convinced that Emma Watson had been the caller, but there was no proof of this and he never bothered to pursue the matter. There was only Tom's evidence that an anonymous voice had said, "The police believe you're responsible for the St Xavier's bombing. Take care."

For Tom, 'taking care' meant only one thing — the elimination of Rosemary White, who alone could identify him. He didn't tell his brother Bert about the warning. He wanted no argument. He decided to act himself.

19

THE next day dawned cold and dank. It had been raining ever since midnight in a steady downpour, which by nine in the morning had become a mournful drizzle. Greg White, calling goodbye to his wife and daughter, left his house. He said good morning to the uniformed constable who was trying to shelter under a tree that offered little protection, and told him to go and stand in the porch.

"You can guard us just as well from there," he said. "No one else will be going out this morning. So when you feel like it, ring the bell and tell my wife you could do with a hot drink."

"Many thanks, sir."

The police officer was grateful. He had been on duty since six, and it would be another three hours before he was relieved. He was not a young man and privately Greg wondered if he would be of much use in the event of an attempt to enter the house. But at least he was a symbol of the law. Smiling at the thought, Greg got into his car and started for the College.

Rosemary watched him from her bedroom window. She had needed to visit the bathroom but, having observed the weather, she was glad to get back into bed and snuggle under the duvet. She was feeling much better, and her temperature was normal. Later, she proposed to dress and spend most of the day up, as she had done yesterday. But this required an effort, and for the moment she lacked the energy.

Neither Greg as he drove down the street, nor Rosemary as she watched him go, noticed the blue Mercedes that was parked a couple of hundred yards along the road. The policeman had seen it, but it had not occurred to him to question its presence. Admittedly, Mercedes cars were not that frequent in these North Oxford residential streets mainly inhabited by dons with families and mortgages, but he had only been warned to look out for a white van or a motorbike. No one had mentioned a Mercedes, and no one had told him that such a car had been stolen during the night, or that the man sitting behind the wheel in a chauffeur's peaked cap which hid his sandy hair was other than what he seemed.

Tom Sarson had seen Greg leave the house, and had been relieved that he was alone. He had thought that on such a vile day her father might have driven Rosemary to school. Tom, of course, had no idea that Rosemary had been ill; his plan, such as it was, had been hastily formulated without thought of reconnaissance or discreet inquiry; reasoning and analysis were hardly part of Tom's impulsive nature. He waited, expecting the girl to appear at any minute, though he was beginning to worry. He couldn't understand why she was so late.

Jean White had washed up the breakfast dishes and was about to go upstairs to make the beds. She had decided that it was time for Rosemary to have a bath and get dressed; her routine must start to return to normal now that she had recovered from the bug. But as Jean passed through the hall she saw that the letters she had written the evening before were still lying on the table; Greg, who had promised to post them, had forgotten. She swore under her breath. One of the letters was important.

For Jean had made up her mind that as soon as Rosemary was well enough to travel, the girl must go to stay with Greg's parents, as had been planned. At the same time, she herself would pay a visit to her sister, who lived in Scotland. Greg would have to cope by himself, but she didn't care. He could always move into his rooms in his beloved St Xavier's. She needed to get away from Oxford and find some place where she was not an object of curiosity to friends and strangers, where she could try to relax. And she also knew that she must get away from Greg, if only for a short time. But the letter asking her sister, who had married late and had several small children, if a visit would be convenient, remained on the hall table. She would have to post it herself. For a moment she thought of the phone, but then dismissed the idea; it would be discourteous to confront Isobel with

316

the need for an instant decision.

"Rosemary!" she called up the stairs. "I'm just going out. Won't be five minutes. Your dad forgot the letters."

"OK, Mum."

Jean picked up the mail and went to the cupboard by the side door where the family kept raincoats, boots, Wellingtons and a miscellany of gardening clothes. The postbox was only at the end of the road, and on such a day she didn't care what she looked like. She put on some boots and took down the nearest raincoat. It was an old school mackintosh of Rosemary's which she had abandoned as too short, but it still fitted Jean who was not as tall as her daughter. What was more, it had a hood that would protect her hair. She slipped it on and let herself out of the house.

"Going to the post," she said when she saw the police officer. "I'll make us some coffee when I get back."

"Thank you, ma'am. That would be most welcome."

Shoulders hunched and head bent Jean hurried through the murky drizzle towards the postbox. She was unaware how very like she was to Rosemary, in the school raincoat and with her face hidden. And Tom Sarson had been waiting for Rosemary. He was expecting her to appear and when he saw the figure turn out of the Whites' driveway and come along the pavement towards him, it never occurred to him for a moment that it could be anyone but Rosemary.

He started his engine and jammed his foot hard on the accelerator. As the Mercedes surged forward he was fleetingly pleased with his foresight at having chosen to steal a big and powerful vehicle for the task he had in view.

Without hesitation he mounted the pavement and drove straight at Jean. She had no time even to scream. Nor was the watching police officer, dashing towards her and shouting into his walkie-talkie as he ran, in time to be of any help.

There was merely a dull thud as Jean's body was thrown up on to the car's bonnet and then the screech of brakes as the Mercedes scraped along the wall in front of a house. In a moment Tom had the car under control again. He bounced off the kerb, causing Jean's body to slide into the road, and deliberately drove over her, before speeding away.

He had no idea that he had killed the wrong woman.

★ ★ ★

Dick Tansey, alerted within minutes, faced a situation that was typical of so many cases; after a period of seeming inaction, a sudden spate of activity made it vital for him to make rapid decisions, determine his priorities and delegate.

The Chief Inspector wished that he could be in three places at once. He would have liked to have broken the news of Jean's death to Greg, and helped him cope with the formalities which were always shattering. He would have liked to have been with Rosemary, and so assure himself that she was in no danger. He would have liked to arrest Bert and Tom Sarson, especially Tom, because he sensed that an attack of this kind — irrational and hazardous as it was — was more in keeping with Tom's character than Bert's. In addition, he judged that Tom was the kind of villain who, if cornered, wouldn't hesitate to kill again.

He gave the matter a few moments' consideration, spoke briefly to the Chief Constable, doubled the protection on the Whites' house and sent WPC Robertson there with instructions to stay close to Rosemary and get in touch with the Pulents who, he was sure, could be depended on to give the girl every support. He dispatched Inspector Carey to St Xavier's, knowing that he could trust Carey to be both tactful and sensible. The Sarsons he reserved for himself.

With Bill Abbot driving, Tansey set off for Colombury once more. He was followed by a small convoy of experts, including a van with a sniffer dog. Their purpose was to take Bert and Tom Sarson into custody and if necessary tear apart the Sarsons' house and outbuildings in search of any evidence of the presence of explosives or the means of making an explosive device. It took but a short time to swear out the necessary warrants, but even that delay meant that the Chief

Inspector was out of luck.

His party missed both Bert and Tom. As soon as the police cars reached the house, Meg, hearing them, came out. Her eyes were wide with fear and she clutched the two children to her.

"Is something wrong, Mrs Sarson?" Tansey asked.

"You tell me," she replied. "You've come for Bert, haven't you? And Tom? Well, you're wasting your time. They've gone and it's no use asking me where because I don't know, and if I did I wouldn't tell you."

"When did they go?"

"A while back."

"That's not very helpful."

"It's not meant to be. Bert's my hubby and if you think I'm going to shop him you've got another guess coming."

"Mrs Sarson, around nine o'clock this morning Jean White, the wife of Gregory White, was deliberately run down by a car and killed. It was murder."

"Jean White? And she's dead? Oh Christ!" There was no doubting Meg Sarson's distress.

"Jean White, yes. Is that what surprises

321

you, Mrs Sarson? Were you hoping the victim would be her daughter, Rosemary?"

"I wasn't hoping it would be anyone. And I'm sure Bert wasn't. It wasn't him! He was here at nine o'clock. He's only just — "

"Just left? And Tom?"

"He's left too."

"OK." Tansey paused, considering. "We'll go into that in a moment." He gestured to Abbot. "Get all the wheels in motion, Sergeant. Circulate their descriptions and let's pull them in as soon as possible."

"Yes, sir. The white van's here but the motorbike isn't."

"Good." Tansey turned back to Meg Sarson. "Mrs Sarson, even if you had no prior knowledge of this crime, there's such a thing as being an accessory after the fact, so you'd be well advised to cooperate with us. I want to question you further, and I've a warrant for my men to search your premises. All right?"

"Yes," she said grudgingly. "You'd better come into the kitchen. The old man's there and I'm not having him frightened by your lot."

They trooped into the house, and Tansey's men dispersed. The Chief Inspector found himself in a large pleasant kitchen, warm and comfortable and obviously the centre of family life. Mr Sarson was sitting in a wicker chair in front of an open fire, and the two children immediately ran to him. It had all the appearance of a happy scene until Meg Sarson ruined it.

"Here's that Chief Inspector Tansey again, Pa. And more trouble."

"There's always trouble," said the old man gloomily, "always has been, ever since our Steve died." He ignored Tansey. "It's the young 'uns you must care for now, Meg. There's hope for them."

"Sure, Pa." Meg sat herself at the long scrubbed wooden table, and gestured to Tansey to sit opposite her. "Go on," she said. "Ask your questions."

Perhaps partly because of her father-in-law's admonition, and partly because she was resigned to what she feared was about to happen, Meg Sarson became reasonably cooperative. Tom had arrived home on his motorbike about ten o'clock that morning; she didn't know how long he had been out. He had filled his saddle-bags with plastic carriers that she guessed contained a few clothes and personal belongings. Then he had a brief talk with Bert, said a hasty goodbye to everyone and left. She had no idea where he planned to go.

Tansey believed her. "And Bert?" he said.

Meg sighed. "Bert came to me," she said. "He was upset. He told me that everything had gone wrong, Tom was crazy and had done for them both. He said he loved me, but he couldn't stand life in prison and he wished they'd never found Steve's diary."

"What?" Tansey couldn't suppress his surprise.

"That's how we know about the lies that the Master of his College told about Steve," old Sarson suddenly interrupted.

"Be quiet, Pa!" Meg was sharp. "Yes, Chief Inspector, Steve kept a diary. He hid it under a loose floorboard in his bedroom. Bert discovered it two or three months ago when he started to redecorate the room."

"And that's when they decided to blow up the Master in his Lodgings," said Tansey, and thought that the Sarsons' delay in attempting to avenge their brother had at last been explained.

"I suppose so. They didn't tell me. I knew nothing about it, I swear. If I had, I'd have tried to stop them. It was a mad thing to do."

"You must have guessed afterwards, Mrs Sarson."

"What if I did? What would you have had me do? Bert's my husband. I'd never have shopped him," she repeated.

Tansey didn't press her. "What else did Bert say before he left?" he asked.

"Nothing much. He was in a hurry. He knew after what Tom had told him that you'd soon be on your way here. He just kissed me and said, 'I love you. Take care of Pa and the kids.' Then he went. I didn't even see him go." Her voice broke and tears filled her eyes. "Little Alf had wet himself and I had to change him." She pointed to the smaller of the two children.

"Bert didn't take the van?"

"No. He knew we'd need it and — and he's always been considerate."

"Where's the diary now? I'll have to take it with me. I'll give you a receipt."

"I'll fetch it. It's in my room," Mr Sarson said, as he slowly got to his feet and shuffled from the kitchen, the two children playing around his legs and impeding him.

Meg Sarson looked at Tansey. "What happens now, Chief Inspector? If you take me in, the kids'll have to go into a home, and so will Pa. He's too sick and old to care for them, and there's nobody else but me."

Tansey nodded. He could have commented that the considerate Bert might have thought of the possible consequences for his family before reacting so violently against St Xavier's and its Master, even if he believed some such action was justified on his brother Steve's behalf. But Tansey kept his peace. He too could be considerate, and he accepted that no good would come from charging Meg Sarson. She was no danger to the Whites, and her children would be the main sufferers if she were sent to prison.

"You stay here, Mrs Sarson — at least for the time being. We'll need you as a witness when Bert and Tom are brought in, but otherwise you should be all right, though I can't promise. You'll have to wait and see. I'll leave a police guard with you."

"Ta!" Meg managed a crooked smile. "Here's Pa," she said.

Old Mr Sarson had returned with the diary, which was in fact a collection of exercise books held together with a thick elastic band. He handed the bundle over to the Chief Inspector.

"Thanks," Tansey said. "You'll get these back in due course. Now I must go and see how my men are getting on."

Meg Sarson followed him to the front door, and they were standing together when they heard a dull report.

Immediately a police officer came running from one of the outbuildings. "It's Bert Sarson, sir," he shouted. "He's blown the back of his head off with what looks like a service revolver."

Tansey took the bundle of Steve Sarson's exercise books home with him, and started on them after a quick supper. His wife Hilary had gone early to bed and there was nothing to distract him, but he was tired and he had to force himself to concentrate. It had been a bad day, one of the worst he could remember. There had been two deaths, Jean White's and Bert Sarson's, both of them in his opinion avoidable, as he had had to admit to the Chief Constable in his oral report late that afternoon.

Because he wanted to get a clear picture of Steve Sarson, Tansey resisted the temptation to tackle the books in reverse order, though he was sure that the last of them would be the most relevant. Steve had been methodical and had devoted one book to each of the nine terms he had spent up at Oxford.

As Tansey had expected the books that covered Steve's first two years were of little importance, though they were touching in many ways. They revealed the wonderment and awe of a young man of eighteen suddenly flung into an environment that was alien to him. Reading between the lines, it was clear that St Xavier's — small and new, and therefore a little exclusive and self-defensive, and with few fellow-undergraduates from similar backgrounds — had not been the ideal choice for a boy like Steve.

Nevertheless, he had worked hard. He had enjoyed the work and he had been determined to get a good degree. His work had also provided him with a safe haven, where he need have no fear of doing the wrong thing; he had been lucky in having Greg White, whom he liked and admired, as his tutor. But White, though he had probably tried, had been unable to save the boy from various embarrassments, such as Fairchild's amusement when he had mistaken the head porter, Dobson, for a don, or Lady Pinel's obvious disdain when he had upset a plate of cakes at one of her tea parties for undergraduates.

He had joined several clubs, but by the end of a couple of terms had more or less abandoned them. He wasn't interested in politics or religion or sport and, though he enjoyed some meetings of an experimental theatre club he met no kindred spirits there. He had never found it easy to make friends and he had little spare money, which didn't help. Nevertheless, it was clear from what he had written that he was enormously proud of being up at Oxford, and that the place lost none of its magic as time went on.

During this period his social life had been virtually nil, but everything had changed at the beginning of his third year, when he was allocated to a different staircase, and found himself in a set of rooms opposite those of Peregrine Courcey. Why Courcey should have befriended him was a mystery, but one that no longer bothered Steve once he had met Hugh Fremont and Amanda Hulton. From then on he seemed to have lived in a dream world.

It was after midnight when Tansey reached Steve's last exercise book, with its account of Steve's final term. Inevitably the dream had come to an abrupt end. Amanda had merely laughed at his proposal of marriage. She had treated it as a joke and told Fremont and Courcey about it. Courcey had been kind but blunt: Steve would never be 'one of them'.

Although Steve had been made miserable by this, there was no suggestion that he considered taking his own life because of it. He had found some consolation in a renewed return to his work, which he knew he had been neglecting, and in the kindness of Emma Watson whom he had got to know earlier through a chance meeting in the College library.

Then there had been the stress of his Final examinations, though he had been pleased with the papers. The accusation of cheating had come as a tremendous blow. "I did NOT cheat," he had written several times, and underlined the words. "How could I?" he asked.

Tansey read through these pages several times. He was appalled. Steve Sarson's account of events was fundamentally different from Sir Philip Pinel's. According to Steve, he had been given no chance to defend himself, and no notice had been taken of his denials. Pinel had simply said that denial was useless; the senior members of the College had decided that he should withdraw the suspect papers, that he would not be awarded a degree and that he must refuse the teaching post he had been offered at London University — if London did not withdraw their offer first. In return the authorities would be silent about the matter, and would save him and his family from disgrace.

There was absolutely no indication in the diary that Steve had ever admitted his guilt. In fact, he had refused to cooperate with the College authorities. Yet it was clear that, on reflection, though he knew he had *not* cheated, he also realized that it would be difficult to convince anyone who mattered that he had just been lucky in the topics he had chosen to revise. He remembered the subjects Emma had suggested, but of the three that had turned up he had himself already marked down two for special treatment, and anyway Emma could not possibly have had any inside knowledge. He was innocent, he repeated, and one day, please God, someone would find the diary, and the truth would become known. In the meantime he had no choice. He couldn't face the disgrace with which the Master had threatened him, and he wouldn't make an effective admission of guilt by doing what the Master demanded. There was only one way out.

Tansey shut the last exercise book as the clock struck two. It was lucky, he thought, that Steve Sarson would never know the cost of his vindication.

20

IT was several months before Tom Sarson came to trial. He had been recognized in a public house by an observant off-duty police officer in Birmingham, some two weeks after he had disappeared. Ironically, the day he was arrested was the day of Jean White's funeral; his brother Bert had been buried the day before.

Tom Sarson was brought back to Oxford, and formally charged with the murder of Jean White and the attempted murder of Sir Philip Pinel. The DPP had decided that Dr Dawson's death, though probably indirectly related to the case, would prove to be merely a complicating factor. Sarson appeared before the magistrates, who remanded him in custody at the request of the police for further inquiries .

The trial, when it eventually took place, lasted for four days, during which time the court was packed, and the media did their best to satisfy the curiosity of viewers and readers, while respecting the fact that the case could not be fully reported until a verdict had been reached. An attempt to have the charges reduced to manslaughter failed, and Sarson pleaded not guilty to both.

Chief Inspector Tansey was convinced that Tom was guilty, but he wished he could be as certain about the verdicts that would be brought in. Unfortunately, in spite of the time the police had had at their disposal and the efforts they had made, very little further evidence had come to light. No positive proof had been found that Tom had been the driver of the Mercedes that had killed Jean. Tom had been lucky. The car, left with the keys in the ignition in a supermarket parking lot, had been driven away by a couple of teenagers, who had crashed it against the wall of a house, where it had burst into flames. The two boys, who had been lucky to escape with their lives, had been scared when they realized they had stolen a murder vehicle, but there was no question of their involvement in the major crime. Nevertheless, the Mercedes had been reduced to a half-burnt-out hulk, and any forensic or other evidence against Tom that might have existed had been destroyed.

It was on the second day of the trial that Tom Sarson, to the annoyance of the young barrister who was defending him at the taxpayer's expense, suddenly announced that, while he had wished no one to die, he was partly responsible for causing the explosions at St Xavier's College. Tansey was not impressed. He was sure that the admission was not the result of remorse, but due to a certain native cunning on Tom's part.

The motive for killing Jean White that the prosecution attributed to Tom — that he had mistaken her for Rosemary, who might identify him as one of the men who had held her family hostage and initiated the bombing of the Master's Lodgings — was admittedly not strong. And the fact that he was now prepared to admit to the bombing seemed, somewhat illogically, to make the denial of the more serious hit-and-run charge more plausible.

As far as the bomb outrage was

concerned, Tansey thought that Tom had reasoned that his best hope was to play on the sympathy of the jury. It could be argued that though the explosion had been relatively large no one had been killed and damage to persons and property had been limited; the prosecution had been prepared to concede that the fatal heart attack suffered by the Senior Tutor could have been coincidental. What was more, the reason for the assault on the Master of St Xavier's and his senior colleagues — an attempt to avenge a younger brother who had committed suicide when falsely accused of cheating in his Final examinations — if not to be condoned, was at least understandable. And Tom could lay the major blame on his brother Bert, who had had the expertise to make the bomb.

It was also advantageous to the defence that Sir Philip Pinel, when he was called as a prosecution witness, did not appear as a sympathetic character. He toyed with the truth, he blustered, and he showed little regard for anyone except himself. He was not given an easy time by the defence, but he was not ill-prepared for the fact that he might well have to face a potentially damaging cross-examination. Tansey had at least seen to that.

The Chief Inspector had pulled no punches when he had insisted on another meeting with the Master. Backed by what he had learnt from Steve Sarson's diary, and supported by Professor Massey-King — who had been horrified by the relevant information that had been passed on to him — Tansey had been blunt.

Sir Philip, he had claimed, presumably out of a desire to avoid a scandal, had bullied Steve Sarson, had threatened his career and his family, and had given him a completely false impression of the situation. Steve had been *suspected* of cheating — no more than that; he had not been convicted by the Master and the Senior Fellows of St Xavier's from the evidence of his work, as Pinel had told him. He had *not* admitted his guilt, as Pinel later maintained. On the contrary, even after he had decided to kill himself, he had sworn that he had not cheated. The law made no mention of death-bed denials rather than death-bed confessions, but the last entries in Steve's diary were the nearest approach to such a denial as the jury were likely to come across.

In his interview with Tansey, Pinel had blustered. He had pointed out that it was Sarson's written words against his personal testimony but, reminded that on the witness stand he would be under oath, he had tempered his attitude. And what Professor Massey-King said to him, or what influence he brought to bear Tansey was never to know, but the Chief Inspector was delighted to read in the *Oxford Mail* some time after the trial that Sir Philip Pinel was resigning his post as Master of St Xavier's at the end of the Trinity Term to become the head of a minor university in Mid-West America.

But if Pinel's evidence and personality raised some sympathy for Steve's brother Tom among the jury, Greg White and Rosemary cancelled it out. They were excellent witnesses, clear, composed, and they showed no sign of vindictiveness in spite of what they had suffered. Tansey was delighted with the impression they made — especially Rosemary.

"Wasn't she wonderful, Chief Inspector?" Tony Pulent said.

"Absolutely splendid," Tansey agreed.

He had met the Whites and their small party — Tony Pulent and his mother and Ailsa Mackay with the Bursar, Peter Lacque, who had attended the trial each day — as they all left the court by a side door to avoid the media. He was pleased to see that the Whites had plenty of support.

"How do you think it's going, Chief Inspector? Or is that not a fair question?" Greg White asked; he was looking drawn but not unhappy.

"It's difficult to tell," Tansey said. "One never knows with a jury. Let's hope this is a sensible lot."

"How much longer do you think the trial will last?"

"With any luck it should be all over tomorrow."

Tansey was proved right. The judge's summing-up was damaging, and the jury were out for only three hours. Then, to the Chief Inspector's relief, they brought in a unanimous verdict of guilty on both

340

counts. The next day Tom Sarson was sentenced to life imprisonment for the murder and fifteen years for the bombing, the sentences to run concurrently. An appeal was ultimately denied.

However, the long shadow cast by Steve Sarson's death was not altogether bleak and sombre. Some three months after the conclusion of the trial Chief Inspector Tansey went into an antique shop in Charlbury to buy his wife a birthday present. To his surprise he was met by Emma Watson. Yes, she explained, she had decided to go into business for herself, and had taken on Meg Sarson as an assistant. Meg lived above the shop with her two children and the old man. "I was fed up with teaching," Emma said. "I've always been interested in antiques and Meg's got some knowledge of the second-hand furniture trade. And we're doing well." She hesitated, then added, "Besides, I felt I owed Steve something."

"Good for you," said Tansey.

Through his growing friendship with Greg and Rosemary, Dick Tansey maintained some contact with St Xavier's. He was pleased to be told later in the year that Peter Lacque was to marry Ailsa Mackay.

As far as the Whites themselves were concerned, though they both mourned Jean, and especially the manner of her death, neither — not even the seventeen-year-old Rosemary appeared to have suffered any lasting ill-effects from their traumatic experiences; Tony Pulent's continuing understanding and support were a great help. Greg's life returned gradually to normal, as he found that St Xavier's, having settled down under a newly-elected Master, was a much happier place where he could continue to enjoy his work; in the following year he completed his *magnum opus* on Milton.

"All in all, a satisfactory case," concluded Tansey, and the Chief Constable concurred.

THE WILDERNESS WALK
Sheila Bishop

Stifling unpleasant memories of a misbegotten romance in Cleave with Lord Francis Aubrey, Lavinia goes on holiday there with her sister. The two women are thrust into a romantic intrigue involving none other than Lord Francis.

THE RELUCTANT GUEST
Rosalind Brett

Ann Calvert went to spend a month on a South African farm with Theo Borland and his sister. They both proved to be different from her first idea of them, and there was Storr Peterson — the most disturbing man she had ever met.

ONE ENCHANTED SUMMER
Anne Tedlock Brooks

A tale of mystery and romance and a girl who found both during one enchanted summer.